Twisted Tales From The Northwest

Twisted Tales From The Northwest

Star Lady Tales Book 1

Mari Collier

Published 2015 by Creativia
Paperback design by Creativia (www.creativia.org)
ISBN: 978-1518766992
Cover art by Creative Paramita
http://www.maricollier.com/

Contents

Good Sam

I first met Charles A. Hinderson at a little restaurant in Fall City where I like to eat after doing some steelhead fishing. Charles was all dogged out in a tweedy suit, preppy sweater, and a white shirt. He had come in to ask directions, but now was using his fist to pound the counter while he shouted at the cashier. His black hair was waved back and cut short on the neck. His nose was like his body: long and lean. It set well in the high boned face with the dark eyes. His ruddy complexion darkened as his frustration mounted over the cashier's directions.

"They keep changing the road!"

"Sir, it's been changed for years," replied the young cashier and she rolled her eyes at anyone who was watching.

I noticed the bright flush extending from his neck to his brow and decided to help. I've always had a penchant for being a Good Samaritan. It's undoubtedly my parents fault for naming me Samuel B. Goodfellow. I laid the bill and money on the counter and reverted to my Good Sam role. "Come on," I offered. "I'll show you the way."

We walked outside to the only main street in town. A light, fair breeze blew off the Snoqualmie River promising the summer to come. Above the breeze pushed the grey clouds forward as a reminder that the spring rains were still with us. "Are you familiar with this area?" I asked.

"One might say I know it well." His voice was choked with bitterness. "But it's been so long since I left home. I must get to Seattle tonight."

"Where are you parked?"

In response, he pointed to a black, 1936 De Soto. I whistled. It was in excellent condition, the finish like new. It even had the original license plates. Later I would wonder why he hadn't been picked up by the police. Other antique autos have special plates.

"Look, the road right here in front of us is Highway 202. Head west, straight through Redmond. Just stay on 202 until it joins 520 at Redmond. Take 520 across the Evergreen Point Bridge to I-5. That will put you north or south of any area in Seattle." I stopped, noting the wild light dancing in his brown eyes.

"However," I added, "I-90 would probably be a lot easier. You just back out and head in the other direction." I pointed to the end of the street towards the Colonial Inn. "You turn right at the Fall City-Preston Road. Do you remember Preston?"

He nodded in affirmation.

"Good. At Preston the signs will lead you straight to I-90. Turn right to head west into Seattle. You'll go by Bellevue, over Mercer Island and Lake Washington."

"What about the ferry?" he asked, breaking into my speech.

My mouth dropped. Hell, he didn't look that old. "Mister, there hasn't been a ferry there since the forties."

The wind seemed to go out of him. "Anyway," I continued, "I-90 takes you across Mercer Island and Lake Washington. You are now in Seattle and can go any direction you want."

He looked dubious. "Is Empire Way still there?"

"Yeah, only they call it Martin Luther King Jr. Way."

A look of resolution came over his face and he turned to shake my hand. "Thank you. I must be home by nightfall." His grip was firm and warm. Something else I would wonder about later.

His old car roared to life, and I wandered back to collect my change from Suzie, the cashier. "I think I got him steered in the right direction."

"Hah!" Derision bubbled out of her glossed mouth. "He's always going to Seattle. He comes in every six months or so."

"Really?"

"Not only that, but my Grandma used to give him directions. He's been a long time driving to Seattle." She giggled. "It always rains when he leaves."

Rain splattered against my windshield as I left Fall City to take one of my clients grocery shopping. I refused to believe the direction asking male was responsible as it always rains in western Washington.

After my divorce from Velma, I started volunteering as a driver for senior citizens on Saturdays. That way I can control my humanitarian impulses. I have to admit it's a satisfying outlet. Other times, it can be completely unnerving.

Two months after giving Hinderson directions my client, the elderly Mrs. Patterson, had a complete emotional meltdown in my car. Her cat, Mr. Tye, a pet of some twenty-five years had passed. She sobbed out her sad tale, tears rolling over her wrinkled face and liver spotted hands.

"I don't have the money to bury him. The county supported complex for senior citizens doesn't have any yard space to bury him."

Then she really began crying. "I don't even have the strength to dig a hole if there was room. I can't, just can't let them cremate Mr. Tye."

"Mrs. Patterson, I'll be over tomorrow and take care of the situation."

I should have restrained my Good Sam instincts. When I arrived, it was obvious that Mr. Tye had developed a distinct odor. Mrs. Patterson had placed Mr. Tye in a cardboard box and covered him with an old lace shawl. Naturally, I promised to bury Mr. Tye in a peaceful place.

In the privacy of my car, I stuck Mr. Tye's makeshift coffin in a plastic garbage bag and headed east on I-90 to the North Bend area, intending to combine humanitarianism with hiking or fishing. My pole and tackle box were up front.

Unfortunately, it was a warm day and the plastic bag didn't cut the smell as much as I had anticipated. After burying Mr. Tye, I headed back into North Bend to a grocery store for a can of air freshener and a six pack. There was still enough daylight to spend some time at Rattlesnake Lake.

As I started to go into the store, I almost bumped into the lost traveler. He was pacing up and down in front of the payphone like he was expecting it to ring. Like a fool, I said, "Why hello. Did you make it to Seattle?"

He grimaced and shook hands. "No, I took a wrong turn."

Now mind you, this was two months later. That must have been one hell of a wrong turn, but he looked so miserable in that tweed suit in the summer heat that I felt real compassion.

"Look, man, I'm heading up to Rattlesnake Lake. Want to come along? There's always plenty of girls on a day like this."

"Thank you, but I really need to get back to Seattle tonight. Would you be kind enough to explain again? I think the others, the young men and the people with rings in their ears or their noses, they-they're laughing at me."

Well, he was bizarre, but he didn't look stoned or smell of booze, and that innate helpful nature of mine rose to the fore as I took his arm to position him towards the exit.

"Just drive out of this parking lot and hang a left." I pointed to the street. "Take the street to the light, turn left, and you are headed out of town. The first turn to the right is the I-90 exit. You go up a steep grade and you are on your way home, straight into Seattle."

He grasped my hand again and pumped it up and down. This was becoming a habit. "Thanks! My wife will appreciate this. My name is Charles A. Hinderson."

"Sam Goodfellow," I said in response.

He looked up at the gathering clouds. "Good, there will be rain," he muttered and sprinted for his antiquated automobile.

I went inside and bought some beer and jerky. When I came out, it was raining and the wind blowing. After wasting a summer's afternoon on a dead cat and Charles A. Hinderson, the doubts about pursuing my humanitarian ways became overwhelming. I took a good look in the mirror that night and decided that since my eyes were still blue and my teeth and hair were still intact at almost forty, it was time to devote my leisure hours to more selfish, and hopefully, more productive activities. Retirement would allow time for bettering the world and helping my fellow humans.

This new resolve lasted for two weeks. Friday night after work, I swung into one of Redmond's large discount stores for some new DVDs. The weather had been A-1 for a western, Washington summer. Lazy, sunny days with a couple of showers tossed in just to remind you of the normal weather. It promised to be a great weekend for getting together with your buds for sports or a barbeque.

I walked out of the store loaded with the DVDs and some speakers I didn't need when who should I see but Charles A. Hinderson stopping people and asking the way to Seattle. His agitated manner and wild gestures were beginning to worry people and I knew it wouldn't be long before somebody called the cops.

"Hey, Charlie, how's it going?" I yelled.

He left off trying to grab this old guy's arm and stared at me with bewilderment. Finally his brow cleared and the brown eyes gleamed with recognition. "Sam, I've got to get to Seattle tonight." He gasped the words out as he tried to pump my hand.

One of the speakers dropped to the cement. Later, I discovered it had cracked. We retrieved the box and walked to my car.

"Where are you parked this time," I asked.

He pointed a couple of lanes over. As we walked I started to describe how to get to Seattle and changed my mind.

"Look," I offered, "I'll be glad to lead the way into Seattle. Just follow me. Remember, once we're out of this lot, we'll need to keep to the right to go south."

The look of gratitude on his face was payment enough for me. I waited for him to pull up behind me, and then we started edging out of the lot. Redmond is one of those fast-growing, urban centers with unbelievable traffic congestion. At least we were turning onto 202 to go right. 202 is a four lane state route with a middle lane for left turns or merging to the right in heavy traffic. Good ole Charlie, however, managed to merge into the left lanes.

You guessed it. He turned left onto Avondale Road and headed straight north, not south. God knows where he thought he was going, but I certainly didn't, and there was no way in that traffic to get back to him. Not that I wanted to as I was heading for Bellevue, not home. By the time I had gone one-half mile, it was pouring rain. That slowed the traffic even more. One hour later, I finally made it home. With luck, I'd never see Charles A. Hinderson again.

That episode should have been enough to curtail my Good Sam efforts forever. I began writing scathing letters to the editor of the local paper about the mistaken do-gooders of the world and started to attend the concerts, movies, and literary readings that I had given up to better mankind. True, I was using these venues as a way to hook up with a woman, but what better way to meet someone who is looking for a footloose, under forty (all right, just barely), goodtime Charley. Scratch that. Make it Sam, Sam Goodfellow.

On the last, long weekend of summer, I headed to Black Diamond's Labor Day Festival. It's a nice little town, nestled in a wooded valley. There was to be a parade, a Soap Box Derby, and an assortment of games and rides. Just the place to be when the temperatures are moderate, the crowd friendly and spaced out instead of a mass of humanity pressed together pretending that they are enjoying themselves.

I opened a can of cold beer at their outdoor café and sat at a table while looking around watching and waiting for an opportunity to meet the opposite sex. I started to make eye contact with a couple of unattended females. Who cares if they were over thirty or forty? They looked self-sufficient and in no need of being rescued from anything but lack of male companionship: Just my type of humanitarianism. The brunette had deep, deep blue eyes and a dimple when she smiled at me. I started to saunter over when someone grabbed my arm and dumped half of my beer.

"Sam, thank God I found you. I'm really desperate this time." Charles, the lost wayfarer, still dressed in his tweed suit, looked haggard as perspiration poured off him.

"My right front tire is flat, and no one in this provincial place can fix a tube tire. Can you believe that?" His voice rose hysterically, and the two women began edging away. He groaned when he saw where my concern was centered. "They were right. No one can help me."

He looked ready to weep; not cry, weep. Something twisted in my gut overriding any resolve to remain aloof as the world began clouding over. I looked upward. Clouds were forging over the Olympics. So much for a rainless weekend, but in western Washington, who expects a rainless weekend?

Charles was walking away, shoulders slumped, a truly abject, beaten man. I was hooked.

"Hey, Charlie, wait up a minute. Let's go take a look at your tire."

Tears glistened on his cheeks as he shook my hand. We walked through the parking lot and down the street with Charlie jabbering about how he needed to get to Seattle tonight. I looked at the car when we arrived, and sure enough, right front tire, flat to the pavement.

"I've used up all the spare patches I had on other flats. They say there's nothing to do but wait until Tuesday when some place up by Duvall opens, and I haven't the money or the means to get there. Sam, my wife is going to be worried sick."

I considered. He certainly had no ability to head toward Seattle even with his auto running. "How long have you been gone?" I asked.

"I don't know. I just know that it has been too long. She might even be tired of waiting." His eyes were black with worry and he kicked at the offending tire. "It was all right as long as I could keep moving."

"Well, let's grab something to eat and I'll take you into Seattle and drop you off by your door." The magnanimity of my offer surprised me. The twinge of regret I felt over the dark-haired beauty was to be obliterated by his gratitude.

Charlie looked stunned. His eyes bugged. His cheeks blew in and out as he rubbed his hand over his forehead. "I'm not sure, but I don't think I should let you."

He was a man totally incapable of making a decision. "Sure you can."

I used his elbow to propel him back to the parking lot. "Here's my car. We'll grab something at the first fast food stand we see."

I shoved him in and rushed around to the other side. Charlie was going home, and I would be rid of him. "You can call the towing company when we get there."

We drove off in silence and stopped long enough to buy chicken and jojos from some orange painted stand. By then, rain was hitting the windshield.

Charlie wolfed down the food and wiped his hands when he finished. "Thank you. I've never had those."

I stared at him. Charlie was definitely different. "Charlie, how long has it been since you've eaten?"

"I'm not sure," he admitted. "The first week, I had some sandwiches and candy bars. Then I ran out of money." He rubbed his hand over his forehead. "It seems like forever, but yet it feels like it was only yesterday since I took this car."

"You mean that is not your car with the flat?"

"Well, no. I had a 1934 Chevrolet, but it overheated and wouldn't start again. I was up in the Cascades returning from Ellensburg where I'd taken a wrong turn so I was later than planned. There wasn't too much traffic, but it was hot, maybe ninety-five, a hundred, I don't know." He paused and then continued in his confused, rambling way.

"This car, the one you've seen, was coming up from North Bend, and the man stopped to help. We pushed my car off to the side, and then he collapsed. He was a heavy man, but I tried to get him over to the side and loosen his tie." Charlie's shoulders slumped even more as he turned to me. I took a quick glance, and I could see wrinkles starting at the corner of his eyes and mouth.

"It was useless," Charlie continued. "He was dead." Charlie shuddered. "Do you know how quickly a body can feel cold and lose its warmth?

"There was no way I could help him, but I had to get to Seattle. I did put him in my car to protect his body from the animals, and then I drove his car to North Bend. I meant to stop for help, but somehow I just kept driving."

Hair was rising on the back of my scalp. Was I driving a madman? Charlie looked harmless; a man beaten down by events. He hadn't killed the man, but he certainly must feel guilty. Suddenly I realized that rain was cascading down my windshield. I turned on the wipers.

"You know, it was raining just like this when I left," Charlie muttered. "My wife, Julie, didn't want me to go, but I laughed at her, and I told her it could rain like this forever. She was to look for me in a week when it would be raining just as hard. Strong men and the Devil can travel in bad weather forever. It was a joke."

He hid his face in his hands while he paused for breath. Bitterness was in his voice when he spoke again. "I've been so lonesome. There's never anyone to talk with except when I ask for directions or pick up a hitchhiker like today."

To get his mind on something different, I asked, "You said you picked up a hitchhiker. What happened to him?"

"I have no idea. He's wandering around that town we came from. I thought maybe he could give me directions, but all he did was lead me further away from Seattle. He lit something called a joint, and the smoke made me dizzy. That's when the tire went flat. He wouldn't even stay around and help me. What ingratitude!" Charlie clenched his fist and pounded his knee. "That's how most people are. They give wrong directions and then they laugh at you."

All my questioning had made him more negative so I flipped a DVD into the stereo. Nothing too loud and wild; it was just a Fleetwood Mac rocking oldie. The music went out and filled the spaces.

He clapped his hands over his ears and screamed, "My God, turn it off!"

I was beginning to regret my generosity and considered letting him out the first chance I had, but the weather interrupted. Normally it's a short run from Black Diamond to I-90, then over Mercer Island, and through the Mount Baker tunnel, but the rain had brought out all the crazies. They wove across the road and scooted between the traffic lanes. All of them making hurrying, yanking movements that endangered life and limb. Autos were hydroplaning on the water coated pavement. Then to compound matters, someone in a Volkswagen slid across the four lanes for the 405 exit.

"Son of a bitch! Did you see that idiot?" I didn't expect an answer, and I flipped the off switch to the music to concentrate on the traffic.

My short run came to an abrupt halt when a loaded gravel truck swept around a car in the tunnel and overturned at the opening that led into Seattle. We screeched to a halt and I prayed that someone wouldn't rear end my rebuilt Camaro.

The truck wheels were slowly spinning to a halt. I shut off the Camaro as the bed and the cab of the truck were effectively blocking all lanes into Seattle. "You might as well relax," I said to Charlie, "while I go check to see if the driver is all right."

Charlie just sat there too stunned to move. His jaw sagged, and the yellow, quartz tunnel lights spewed their glow over his face making a strange, grooved pattern.

"Look, I'll be right back," I said to reassure him, but he made no response. I shrugged and hiked on up.

A couple of other guys were already there. "Is he okay?" I asked.

"Dunno. He ain't moving."

I pulled out my cell phone, moved to the outside of the tunnel, and punched 911. That's me: Good Sam, always prepared and doing what needs to be done.

Medic 1 was there in less than five minutes. So were the cops. They hustled the driver off in the ambulance, but it took the wrecker longer to arrive, and it took even longer to clear the road. I kept hiking back to see how Charlie was doing. After the third time, I stayed with him. He wasn't moving as he had fallen asleep. I didn't want to stay there, but I had to watch. My mind told me it had to be Charlie, but my senses, my intellect, and my guts couldn't accept what was happening. Each time I returned, his dark hair was greyer, his flesh more shriveled and wrinkled. The closed eyes were sinking into the skull, and the thick, dark eyelashes were as white as his hair. At least he was still in the same preppy, tweed suit, and his wing of a nose was still hovering between his wide set cheek bones. What in God's name was happening?

By the time everything was cleared, it was close to four o'clock in the afternoon, and there were huge veins on his gnarled hands. The rain had quit and the sun was back while the clouds retreated into small, grey lumps. Soft, golden light glistened against the wet shrubs and trees.

The sound of traffic woke Charlie and he rubbed his hand across his eyes. "Where are we?"

"Seattle." I eased the car down the first ramp to head to Martin Luther King Jr. Way.

"It can't be," he shrilled. I could sense him turning first towards me, then towards the street. "The houses, the streets, they're wrong. I told you, I live just off Empire Way."

"Charlie, they changed the name some years ago."

"No, it's a fine, new neighborhood. It's not like this: not all these strange, dark, looking people. Who are they anyway?" His voice was growing surly.

"Probably Vietnamese, Koreans, Ethiopians, Mexicans, you know, all the new people who have immigrated."

I could almost hear him shaking his head. "No, I don't know," he muttered.

"Look, I don't have time to explain. What's your address?"

"You need to turn on South Wadworth Place, but it's useless. We're not on the right street."

I ignored him. "Do we turn right or left?"

"You turn right," said Charles. He clammed up, but kept staring out of the window at an alien world.

11

I was driving slowly, but I barely had time to make the turn. If it had been dark and raining, I would have missed it. As I turned on South Wadworth Place, I asked, "How far?"

"Just a couple of houses," he muttered.

"Look, Charlie, I want you home as bad as you do. Hell, I've blown my whole day." I was afraid to mention that I'm driving around with someone who metamorphosed before my eyes. He could go ballistic on me.

Suddenly he straightened. "There! There! See that sign?" His voice had taken on a note of awe and he was stabbing one blue veined finger towards a driveway almost obliterated by high laurel shrubs. Over the driveway, anchored to white, ornamental railing swung the sign: Hinderson's

It was hard to believe. We were but a few feet from getting Charles home. I pulled the car up into one of those old-fashioned driveways with two parallel strips of concrete, and gravel running down the middle. Other than the outside shrubbery, the place looked like new. There sat a neatly painted, white bungalow, grass clipped, and trees and shrubs looking like they had been set out about five years ago. Any other place in this part of Seattle would have had rhododendrons and lilacs towering as high as the trees.

There was no car in front of the house, and it was still too early for lights. It looked cool, quiet, and serene. Charles had his hands clasped in front of him like a man praying. Hell, he was praying. I could see his lips moving.

We walked up to the door. Charles was moving like a man sleepwalking, unable to believe that his quest was over. I looked, but couldn't find a doorbell, and used the brass knocker. Somewhere a squirrel chattered, but the house remained silent. I banged away with the knocker again and let Charles take my place.

The door swung open revealing a lovely, young woman with light brown hair pulled back into a bun. It was no wonder Charles had been so intent on getting home. Her eyes were Puget Sound blue and she had an incredible peaches and cream complexion. The housedress covered with a bib apron couldn't hide the form that swelled, tapered, and swelled again. What she wore on her feet, I couldn't tell you. I wasn't looking at feet.

Her blue eyes looked up at Charles. "Yes?" A slight frown wrinkled the smooth brow as she pursed her pink, full lips.

"Julie, I—Julie," Charlie's words were strangled and half fell out of white pinched lines that formed his mouth.

"Do I know you, sir?" The voice was low, almost husky.

Charlie was gasping, his knees were trembling, and he put his hand on the doorjamb to brace himself. That's when he noticed the old man's hand and the skinny arm covered with white hair protruding from his sleeve cuff. A look of horror came over his face. He put his arms up and surveyed both of his old man's hands as disbelief washed over his face. I caught him as his legs buckled.

"Ah, we're looking for Charles Hinderson's place," I blurted out.

"Charles isn't home right now. I'm sorry, but I can't invite you in. The last time a deliveryman came in, things seemed to change."

Her calm voice was maddening. "Well, uh, when do you expect him?" I asked.

"Charles should be home anytime now, perhaps with the next rainstorm. He called me a while back and explained how and why he was delayed. To be safe, I'm not to go out until he returns."

"Look, my friend needs a doctor. Maybe we could use your telephone."

She shook her head. "I'm truly sorry about your friend. He reminds me of someone. If you have business with Charles, you'll have to call our lawyer, Mr. Sherwood Allen. He's located in Seattle."

She smiled pleasantly waiting for us to leave. When no words or movement came from us, she closed the door.

By this time, Charles was able to stand on his own two feet, and I released my grip. "That was your wife, right?" I asked.

He nodded, too shaken by the turn of events to speak.

My mind was whirling. For some reason she hadn't changed any more than Charles had until he left his car. It wasn't natural, but then nothing about Charles was natural. "We could break down the door," I suggested.

"No, no. That would frighten her. She's too genteel."

I took him by the arm and led him back to the car. "When did you call her and tell her not to go anywhere?"

"It was shortly after I acquired the De Soto that I'm driving. I'd made it all the way into Seattle, but I'd picked up a lame hitchhiker. To ease my conscience about the dead man, I guess. He wanted to catch a ferry to British Columbia so I took him down to the docks. By then the rain had stopped and the fog was rolling in. After I dropped him off, I took a wrong turn and wound up in Ballard."

Charles was weak from shaking, so I opened the door and shoved him in. He had enough strength to stretch up and look in the rear view mirror. What he saw made him bury his head in his hands and groan.

I got in and backed down the driveway. I was totally perplexed. What the hell was I supposed to do now? I had tried to get away from the elderly crying, and now one was in my car and he had no one else in the world.

After a time Charlie raised his head. "I must have been away from home a long time." It was a statement, but still a question.

"I figure it's been over seventy years." No use lying to the man.

He stared ahead. "But Julie hasn't changed, not much."

I considered the possibilities. "What did you tell her when you called the last time?"

"That everything was going wrong since I became lost. That it was possible the police would be looking for me and that she should stay in the house, have everything delivered, and hire someone to do the yard work that she couldn't do herself. We have enough money. My family had given us good stocks and bonds, and she had inherited the house from her grandmother. As long as she stayed home with everything the same, then I could find my way back, but it would be raining hard when I did arrive."

"That's it, Sam! Don't you see? Take me back to that car. I'll get that tire repaired somehow and go back to her just like I promised."

I was silent for a while, but in a crazy way his words made as much sense as anything else that had happened.

"Okay, Charles, but we'll make one stop for that tire."

True to my word, we stopped at one of the chain auto stores and picked up a repair kit for bicycle tires and one other purchase. Charles stayed in the Camaro. He was probably afraid he would see his reflection again.

When I returned, I tossed him the smaller package and put the larger one in my trunk. Charles put the contents of the sack in his suit pocket. "There'll be less contamination this way," he explained. "And, Sam, I'll fix the tire by myself. It has to be that way."

Black clouds were scudding around the moon when I pulled up under the street light by Charles's De Soto. The day's heat had vanished and cool fall winds slid across the valley floor promising an oncoming rain storm.

I didn't wander off to look for that sweet brunette. Instead I drank another beer and watched Charles vigorously attack the tire like a younger man. When he finished, he wiped his hands on an old rag and dusted off his trousers. He came over to shake my hand.

"Whoa, contamination," I reminded him. "You were right Charles. You only look about fifty now."

Relief swept over his face and he cracked a wry grin. "Well, this is goodbye then."

"Not quite," I answered and held up the tow chain I had purchased. "This time when I take you to Seattle, you can't make a wrong turn."

Disbelief raged across his face and tugged at his voice. "But, Sam, I have to wait for the rain."

I paid no attention. "Here, secure your end because I am not touching your car except to make sure it is on correctly. Just keep your motor running, your lights on, and your gear in neutral. I'm betting by the time we're there, it will be pouring rain."

There's nothing in life like being wrong. It didn't pour. Whoever or whatever Charles's arrogant dare about strong men and the Devil traveling forever in the rain antagonized emptied the oceans on us. By the time I turned onto Martin Luther King Jr. Way the rain was jumping from the street to the hood and the wipers were having difficulty keeping the windshield clear. In the eerie, rain-darkness, the street lights seem to change to the old fashioned ones. When Charles blinked his lights, I turned on the street that I hoped was South Wadworth Place and pulled up to the curb after passing two or three houses.

The rain soaked our clothes through while we disengaged the tow chain. Charles's teeth were chattering, but I couldn't tell if it was from the rain or the improbability that he was actually home.

"Now we push." How was I to know that these were my last words to him?

It was all I could do to keep from slipping to my knees with the water gushing down from the sky and overflowing in the street. Catching sight of much smaller laurel bushes by the driveway didn't help my equilibrium.

When we were in front of the house, Charlie hit the horn. Somehow Julie heard it over the rain beating on everything, and she turned on the lights. It was insane, but Charles's plastered down hair was black again.

She came running out of the house and into his arms, the rain molding the flimsy robe to that magnificent body. For the first time, I actually envied him. He stroked away the tears, rain, and hair from her face.

"Sweetheart, I've got to make a telephone call to the police. There's a body up above North Bend. I think his family would want to know what happened to him."

They were back in their world, and I went back to mine without a handshake or a goodbye. Now if anyone asks me for directions, I never answer them. Never!

Customs

I was headachy and hungry after driving all afternoon and night without a break in the drizzling rain to this oceanfront town where grey roiling clouds come boiling downward into the grey rolling waves. Like the sky above the wood buildings had weathered to grey. The buildings gave no evidence of paint ever gracing their walls. They were simply age worn slabs of wood slumping into each other; gaunt, beaten relics from another time forming a backdrop for the grey sidewalks and empty pavement.

Most of the windows flanking the street were unlit and presented blank, empty sockets of despair. They matched the eerie blank, emptiness of the town.

It was eleven o'clock in the morning, Pacific Standard Time. The dreary town and the surrounding scenery did nothing to improve my state of mind. To the south were stunted, wind twisted trees that managed to look black against the black rocks. Salt spray coated their needles, turning their darkened green points to an ashen color. A few wisps of reedy grass gradually faded into the grey sand which sloped and slid into the grey sea. What few boats floated at the quay were in dire need of paint and repair. The very air reeked of rot and decay to create a maleficent odor to match the wisps of dissipating fog. This place was beyond eerie. It was a tragedy that had already happened. I couldn't understand how my brother became enchanted with this place. The back and forth sound of the swishing, crashing waves mocked me and added to the throbbing in my head.

There was one restaurant on Main Street with a wooden EATS sign swaying back and forth in the wind and mist. I pulled up in front of the building and bid my uneasy stomach to quiet down. It was a quick dash into the restaurant, and once inside after closing the door against the weather there was the pleasant surprise of good smelling coffee and cinnamon buns.

The plump, middle-aged lady at the counter was swiping at non-existent dirt and occasionally at her salt and pepper hair. There was a softness in her plumpness as though decay had started on the inside and the skin was but a fragile shell holding her body together. Her doughy face was endowed with a very red nose between closely set red-shot eye whites. Her discolored eyes and puffed bags under them told me she had been crying. She sniffed a couple times and started to get a menu.

"Please don't bother. All I want is a cup of black coffee and one of those nice cinnamon rolls." Rather than look at her while eating, I retreated to one of the booths.

Within seconds the coffee, the bun, a pat of butter, a napkin and a knife were in front of me. While I ate, I spread out the letter I had received. The words were cold and harsh. They told of my brother dying between four or five weeks ago at sea. The boat had drifted aimlessly with its dead cargo of fish and men before being towed into town. A mass burial was to be today as the county had no way to preserve the deteriorated bodies, or monies to send the bodies elsewhere. The cause of death was presumed to have been a virulent fever or virus. To prevent any disease from spreading all were to be buried on today's date by order of a District judge. There would be no viewing due to the deteriorated condition of the bodies. The address of the mortuary and the name and address of the sheriff were included if more information was wanted. None of this made any sense to me. If the culprit of death was an unknown disease, why wasn't the Center for Disease Control (CDC) involved?

The woman reappeared with the coffee. "Care for a warm up?"

"Thank you, yes. This bun is delicious."

The woman sniffed. "It's my ma's recipe. I see you got one of them letters too."

"Yes, I—did you say too? You mean someone in your family was on that ship?"

The woman nodded her head yes. "Ma'am, practically every family in town got one. There isn't anything here but fishing, and now another whole generation is gone."

"Another?" My voice had somehow become a whisper. "This has happened before?"

Her face hardened and she pulled the ticket out of her pocket. "Here. If you want to know more you can go talk to that renegade sheriff that insists everybody has to be buried today. It's wrong. The county's wrong too. They can't be buried today. They should be buried tomorrow." She turned on her heel, marched back behind the counter while fumbling for a hanky and turned her back on me.

I finished the coffee, folded the letter, walked up to the front by the cash register and laid the money on the counter with enough for the tip. "Where would I find this sheriff, and where is the mortuary?"

The woman's face was wet and more doughy looking than ever. Her words fairly snapped out of the pouting lips. "You'll find his office at the end of this street. The mortuary is up the hill from there." She answered without really looking at me.

The fine mist had quit, but I decided to drive down to the end of the block. Where, I wondered, were the people? I had seen no one but the woman at the restaurant. Were they skulking behind their dark windows with some evil intent? Were they plotting to stop the burial? To me this place embodied the evil that killed my brother. This town was old, and perhaps the people were as deteriorated as the buildings. Darrin had extolled its ancient charm in the one letter I'd received from him while he lived here. He liked the rough and easy camaraderie of the fishermen and had purchased a small home. He planned to use his wages from the fishing trip to remodel it. I shuddered at the idea that he would be here forever, and drove into the parking lot at the side of the police station.

This was the only brick building in town, but like the rest of the buildings it was old, the bricks faded, and the wet, black shingled roof glistened into the cloud leaden sky. The entry was a surprise. The double door had a fresh coat of white paint, and the jambs and lintel were wide, giving the appearance of a stateliness lacking in the rest of the buildings. The brass plaque to the right of the door explained to the world that this building had been erected in 1905.

Inside the door, I found a wide room divided into two parts: a waiting area with semi-comfortable blue-green chairs, a table with matching chairs, unlit lamps and several small end tables with magazines. The other area held a desk and built-in dark cabinetry. Dark wainscoting stood underneath the white walls. A chandelier with a golden inverted bowl hung above the heavy oak desk and cast its illumination over the desk and the man sitting on the other side of it. He looked up as I entered.

"Hello, I'm Rose Devon. Your office sent me this letter concerning my brother's death. I desperately want to see him before the burial, and I want more information about his death. Can you help me?"

The sheriff stood and at least (to my eyes) he looked like an everyday person. He was almost six feet tall, a stocky but muscular build, thinning brown hair in a butch cut and wary blue eyes. The blue-grey uniform did nothing to brighten the décor.

"Ms. Devon, I'm Sheriff Malone. I'm sorry we meet under these circumstances. I can direct you to the mortuary, but as far as viewing, that will be up to the funeral director. I warn you, it will not be pleasant. The dead and the boat were too long at sea before being found.

"As for the deaths, we're not exactly sure what happened. Three of the crew members were missing and the boat had been badly damaged by the storm or deliberately vandalized. Whether the men were totally incapacitated prior to the storm, during the storm, or afterward, we'll never know. The storm knocked out all communications and washed through the helm area effectively destroying all electrical equipment. The Captain's log was never recovered. When the Coast Guard boarded the ship, they found one man's partially written letter about the illness. This town is too small to support a doctor, and the county sent over a specialist. The bodies were deteriorated to the point where an analysis of the disease was impossible at this level. Tissue was taken from each body, but to prevent an outbreak of an unknown disease elsewhere, the bodies must be buried within a certain time frame.

"I regret that this information may seem cold and heartless, but county deputies and state troopers will be here this afternoon to keep order. You're entitled to visit the mortuary, but you're on your own. For your own safety, I suggest you leave now."

His mouth was grim, the blue eyes cold. He nodded at me, sat at his desk, and began typing again.

Fury over took me and I shook as I turned to leave. "Thank you, so very much, Sheriff Malone." Sarcasm laced my words. The man was infuriating. He possessed neither sensitivity nor sympathy for anyone suffering bereavement. I slammed the door as I left.

In my haste, I almost bumped into an elderly man walking across the parking lot. He wore a dark, long cloth coat, a grey fedora and a white scarf wrapped neatly around his neck and tucked underneath the lapels. The black gloved hands folded over his cane as he looked at me. His eyebrows were white, but the wrinkled skin seemed to have a white hoar over the pink underneath. He, like the clothes he wore, was from another era, and the words he spoke proved it.

"I see our Sheriff's winning personality has offended yet another newcomer. Are you all right, my dear? May I be of assistance?"

I took a deep breath and steadied myself. "I'm sorry. I wasn't looking where I was going. Thank you for the offer, but according to the lady at the restaurant, all I need to do is drive up this hill and I'll find the mortuary somewhere along the street."

"It's really quite a short stroll. I was headed that way myself to check on Lillian. It's rather depressing in there right now, and she can't leave. Fortunately, our townspeople are not blaming her."

"Why on earth would they blame her?"

"The burial today has put everyone on edge. It's but thirty-nine days since the date on the letter started by the last living crewman. They shouldn't be buried until after the fortieth day." He smiled at me and straightened. "If you will accompany me, I'll be happy to be your guide."

His words were utterly cryptic. What would forty days have to do with anything? At least the rain had not started again, and I walked beside him. If someone his age said it was a short walk, I saw no reason to waste the gasoline.

I looked up the street as we came out of the parking lot. About half-a-block up the street a tall, set on posts, white neon sign showed the green lettering: EVERGREEN REST. A low, sprawling building that had once seen white paint was set back off the street.

"If you don't mind my asking, why must you wait forty days before burial?" Because of his cane and his age, our pace was not rapid.

"It is a custom our town instituted when a ship carrying the original settlers in 1858 wrecked off the coast and continued when a horrible logging accident killed a number of our men in 1876. Anytime a major catastrophe claims so many lives, the prescribed forty days are honored. Only World War I and World War II prevented us from observing it. Now this!" His voice became grim.

"Was the custom begun because embalming wasn't practiced and people held a wake for a certain length of time?"

"Oh, no, embalming was available here by 1876. It gave people time to grieve and to console one another."

"When was the last time this community was struck by disaster?"

"It was 1974. The sea is a cruel master. A fishing vessel was over-turned on the high seas. A Coast Guard cutter was able to retrieve the ship, but the bodies were lost. The state and the county weren't so involved with a remote area then. Ah, here, we are. Allow me." He stepped forward and pulled opened the dark, heavy door.

The stench hit my nostrils as we stepped into the front room. It was faint but undeniable, and I wondered how anyone could remain here all day.

The carpet was a subdued celery color. The walls were white with wide spaced green stripes running from floor to ceiling. Several landscapes in gold or heavy brown frames were on the walls. The chairs were heavy, dark wood upholstered in a light green. The matching carved tables were artfully strewn with an assortment of magazines and one held the bible.

A probably-in-her-thirties, stout, dark-haired woman emerged from behind one of the closed doors. Her stoutness, unlike the other townswoman, implied strength as she moved with a brisk, athletic ability.

"Welcome, is there any way I can assist you? Oh, Mr. Henry, how thoughtful of you to stop by." She looked like she was about to curtsy, but aborted the attempt. "Is there anything you need?"

Mr. Henry removed his hat. "No, my dear, but this lovely stranger was looking for the mortuary, and it was my pleasure to assist her."

"I'm Rose Devon, sister to Darrin Devon. He is among those who are to be buried today. I would like to see him. I need to know." My throat constricted and I stopped talking before my voice broke. This is not the time for tears, I thought, but the desire to see him had grown stronger with each step I'd taken towards this place.

"I'm Lillian Rawlings." She put out her hand and shook mine. "Are you sure? The smell is even worse back there. We'll need to put on masks and gloves. By the time they were brought here, they were beyond embalming. All I could do was put them and the bags they were enclosed in into the caskets and lower the lids."

My chin jutted forward as I replied, "Where is the mask?"

"We'll need to go in together. I have the list in my office saying who is in each casket and which order they are to be buried. This way, please." She turned and motioned me to follow her.

In her office she handed me a gasmask with an attached bottle of oxygen. "I had to wear these and a complete bodysuit when I worked on them. Any questions before you don that?"

"Why hasn't the CDC been here?"

"They were. They took tissue samples and left. They won't notify me or anyone else unless they find a highly infectious disease."

She demonstrated how to put the mask on and use the oxygen. "We'll need to wear gloves also." Two pair of white plastic gloves were pulled from a box and one pair was handed to me. Then she took a notebook from her desk and donned her own mask before we walked down the hall. She swung open a door to a large room crowded with twenty caskets.

The room was painted white and grey-green drapes were hung at intervals to give the appearance of windows. More landscapes were on the walls. An organ sat in the far right-hand corner and a small stage with a lectern was on the left. Wide doors led to the outside on the right. Subdued recessed lighting made the place look surreal, almost like a barely lit dream sequence. I followed Ms. Rawlings to the last casket on the left. She closed the notebook, placed it on the floor, and used both hands to swing the lid upward. She untied the strings and pulled the bag downward.

In a horror movie, the dead bolt upright. This was worse. That blackened and pink blotched skin, bloated creature could not belong to the handsome, laughing older brother I held in my heart. Instead of bolting upright, he lay there in an unnatural position, his eyes bulging outward, and nothing stirred.

My stomach and heart turned in revulsion. Suddenly, unbidden sobs were coming from my throat. I turned and stumbled towards the door. Behind me I heard the casket close, and then Ms. Rawlings's hand was on my elbow, and she supported me to the door. When we returned to Ms. Rawlings's office, she guided me to the chair and then stripped off her mask and mine.

"I warned you." Ms. Rawlings stuck a box of tissues under my nose and pulled one out. I hurriedly held it over my face. Without the mask, the smell returned, coating every breath, and making me ill.

"I think I need to step outside," I managed weakly.

Ms. Rawlings helped me up and guided my steps. Mr. Henry rose when we entered, stepped to the door, and opened it. He followed us out to the covered walkway. "Do you need anything?"

"Thank you, no." I was pulling in great chunks of wet air. Anything was better than the air inside that building. How did Ms. Rawlings stand it?

Mr. Henry stepped next to me. "Perhaps, Ms. Rawlings, you could bring a chair out here for our visitor."

Within seconds there was a chair for me, and I sat long enough for my head to quit spinning.

Ms. Rawlings and Mr. Henry had stepped back and I could hear them whispering through the fuzziness that seemed to envelope my head and ears. It was something about casket number twenty and black skin and natural skin.

"What? Are you talking about my brother?" My voice was harsh in my pain.

"Yes, I just told Mr. Henry which casket your brother is in, and how it must be the full forty days after seeing him again. I put him in number twenty since he was the newest member of our community. We thought we would have the time to do things properly. We meant no insult to his memory."

My head cleared as she spoke. "I'm sorry," I apologized and stood. Both of them were still watching me closely. "Usually, I'm quite capable."

"Of course you are," replied Ms. Rawlings. "It's the shock of seeing your brother like that."

A line of county patrol cars and vans began arriving. They followed the curving driveway to the rear. "Here they come," muttered Ms. Rawlings. "You'll have to excuse me. I've work to do. Someone has to be there to make sure the right coffin goes into the right grave." She took the chair and hurried inside.

"Well, my dear, would you like me to walk you back to your car?"

"That's kind of you, but I want to go to the cemetery for the burial."

"Why would you do that? There will be no services for your brother until tomorrow, if then." His voice was gentle. "The funeral will be for the ones who would have been among the first to die."

"Excuse me? I don't understand."

"The custom I told you about must be fulfilled. The first ones to die are buried first as there will be one that returns. He will become the leader of the community."

"That's impossible."

"No, my dear, it is possible, and the town will insist its customs are followed. You see no one returned in 1974. The last return was from a mass burial in 1937, and I am so tired. I wasn't a youngster on that sailing trip."

I shook my head in disbelief. The man was delusional. Arguing would get me nowhere. "I need to get to the cemetery before all of the cars."

"My dear, I urge you not to go there. There will be trouble. The townspeople that are left are waiting there. Just Mrs. O'Brien, the restaurant owner, Ms. Rawlings, the sheriff and I are not."

"Why?"

"Mrs. O'Brien used a cell phone to alert the others when she saw the patrol cars go past the restaurant. Ms. Rawlings must be here according to the county. The sheriff must appear to support the county and state laws, and I, well, I am too old to be of any assistance. It won't matter. If it goes well, I will die."

I gritted my teeth. "I was told the cemetery is up this hill. How far is it?"

"Not far at all. Once you are at the top, you are there, but I urge you to return to your car and leave."

There were no words to answer him. Everyone was trying to thwart my need to see my brother buried. Who cared about their superstitions? I swung away and walked up the hill, past the towering firs that lined both sides of the street. The skies remained overcast as though day had never arrived on this forsaken corner of the world.

The street seemed to curve into the wide entrance. A huge wooden sign proclaimed: EVERREST. Surely with their beliefs this was some form of irony. As I entered the property, I noticed the neat graves, the older tombstones, and the crowd gathered at one end. Piles of fresh dirt spaced two feet apart told me where the burials would be. I decided to walk along the side and join the others waiting for the arrival of the vehicles bearing the coffins.

They frowned at me as I approached, and they began muttering in low tones. I stopped, rested against the fence and then edged around them down towards the last gravesite reserved for my brother. Did they think I was a reporter come to infringe on their grief?

Soon a steady procession of vans and patrol cars passed through the entrance headed towards the back. A fusillade of rocks greeted them as the crowd surged forward yelling threats. The townspeople were mostly women and teenagers with the few remaining men; yet the rocks they were throwing were surprisingly large. They managed to stop the procession at the first five graves.

The police turned on their loudspeakers, and a voice began bellowing. "Please step back and cease your activities. We will fire. There are state troopers standing by if you do not listen to reason."

A car pulled in behind the police vans. It was Ms. Rawlings and Mr. Henry. He stepped out of the car and walked forward. As he came abreast of the first police car, he began to speak, his voice young and vigorous. "My fellow townsmen, I have faithfully led you all these years. Another is coming. Please adhere to what I say now; my last command.

"Move back and let the authorities do their job. What will be, will be. I beg you. I want no causalities today."

The stones and rocks slowed and then ceased. The police emerged from their vehicles.

"I thank you, my friends. Please excuse me for I must sit down." He returned to Ms. Rawlings's car and the burials began with the lowering of the coffins.

I edged forward to watch more closely for my brother's coffin. The crowd had backed off; a sullen, grey and black clothed crowd, muffled against the weather and the possibility of more rain. As coffin nineteen was lowered, one of the police shouted, "Where's the other coffin? There's another grave here."

Ms. Rawlings opened her car door and stepped out. She did not approach the officers, but began shouting. "There's no need of another grave today. Our customs are fulfilled. Mr. Henry will be buried there in the normal space of time." She slid into her car, slammed it into reverse and sped back out to the street.

The crowd erupted in shouts and began throwing their remaining stones. Three of the tallest people from the crowd moved in front of me, blocking my way. I tried to get around them, but tripped on a tree root running along the top of the ground and I heard them muttering behind me.

"She shouldn't be here."

"She's an outsider."

"We can't let her tell the world about us."

I tried to rise, but the last I knew a stone hit my forehead and another hit the right side of my head. Pain and dizziness blurred my vision and I remember nothing until waking here. My senses tell me a door has opened and fresh air seems to float into the stuffy place where I lay.

"Right this way, sir." I hear Ms. Rawlings voice.

I hear the muffled sounds of two people walking towards me. Then they are gazing down at me: Ms. Rawlings and a wind tanned, handsome, dark haired man with blue eyes. They stand there for a moment, the proper respectful, sad faces of two mourners. The man leans over and places a white rose on my chest and his words come as a cruel obscenity.

"My sister looks lovely, Ms. Rawlings. I hope Mr. Henry looks as well."

Family Traditions

She drifted slowly upward, the pain a dull, stabbing throb pushing her toward awareness, yet dragging her numbed body back to the recesses of darkness and forgetfulness. She opened her unbandaged eye, not really able to focus, but aware that she was lying in a strange bed, her right arm restrained by a cast, her face half bandaged and her left arm strapped against the railing with tubes and needles protruding from her wrists. Her mouth was dry and puffy. The dryness extending downward into her throat making every cell pulse with desire for liquid, something soothing, slightly salty, and warm, she thought lazily.

The room was small and its white walls gave a false image of space. To her left, she sensed a window and wondered what time of day or night it was. If it were day, were the drapes drawn? Before the panic could overwhelm her, she realized it was night. There was light seeping under the door. It was the bright artificial light of night. Content that there was no danger, she almost drifted backwards to the dark world she had just left, but the pain kept nudging her into wakefulness.

Why do I think I am female? Her mind was working in slow loops, not connecting with useful information.

Oh, yes, she thought. I am female because my name is Valda. No, that's wrong. I changed that. It was my father's Aunt Catryn who named me that, she who had fled Hungary before World War I and started the family business. It was she who gave me that old-fashioned

29

Slavic name. I am Valerie, Valerie Trepas. No ancient crone could dictate who she, Valerie, would be.

Her identity was now established, but where was she? For a moment she panicked as shades of yellow and gray exploded in her mind, blocking any thought process. Once more she opened her uncovered eye, gasping in pain and confusion. Attached to the needles and tubing that were lodged in her wrists, she saw two plastic bags suspended on a metal frame. Liquid was slowly dripping into her body. One liquid appeared yellowish, the other was blood. She could smell it.

Now it made sense. She must be in a hospital, but how did they know her need for blood? And how did she get here? And why was she able to see so well in this half-light? She relaxed against the pillow. Think, Valerie, think, she told herself.

She could hear movement outside. It sounded like someone pushing a cart. It seemed to halt and she could hear another door open and she fought the blackness hovering in the background. Awareness slowly returned. She knew she had been awake earlier, before they brought her to this room. There had been asinine questions.

"Who is your primary care provider? Where is your family? Who is your insurance carrier?"

Bah! Stupid creatures. She had been unable to respond and all she could do now was to remain here and endure the pain. Once again she forced her mind back to recall how she came to be here.

Yes, there had been an accident. Valerie remembered hurrying home to be there for Robert's arrival when some maniac came blasting off the paved, county road, slamming her vehicle into a waiting hemlock. She remembered flooring the brake pedal before everything blacked out.

Now her head was throbbing again. No, not throbbing, it hurt, hurt damned hard. It was too difficult to recall anything else. Outside a cart stopped and someone entered the room, upping the light volume. Valerie tried to raise her hand for protection, but she was tied on one side and encased on the other. She turned her head and moaned, biting at her lips, wishing for the taste of....

"There, there," came a soothing voice. "You've been in a bad accident. This is your second day here and now we are going to take your temp. Then if you want, we can give you something for your pain."

She inserted a probe into Valerie's ear and then clamped something on her upper arm. "We need to take your blood pressure too."

Valerie would have preferred to pull all of the painful, helpful things off, but she was aware enough to sense that for now she was dependent on the good graces of those who were caring for her. Since most of them were hired at menial wages, they were quite capable of behaving in snide ways if a patient became too obnoxious. No, it was better to wait until she was strong enough to move.

The pressure relaxed on her arm and there came the noise of a keyboard. The woman moved to check the fluids, "Hmming," at the blood bag and stopping to check the chart. "Yes, I see you are to have that."

"Well, how are we feeling now?" The woman's cheerful noise scratched at Valerie's nerves. Valerie would have preferred to tell the woman exactly how she felt and how the woman would soon feel, but instead whimpered, "I hurt and I'm confused. Where am I?"

"You are at Providence Hospital."

"What time is it?" Valerie was ready to panic again.

"It's a little after five a.m. I go off duty at six a.m."

Valerie wondered why the woman would think she would need to know the latter, but wisely held her tongue.

The woman continued. "Paul will be here to care for you next. I'll move the communicator closer to your fingers. Can you see it? Just push the red button if you need assistance for the bed pan or anything. The doctor doesn't want you to be up just yet. Would you like the drapes open?"

"No!" Valerie gasped. "The light above, the sunlight hurts my eyes, my eye I mean."

"Of course, it does, dear. You've had a nasty bump."

"You said I could have something for the pain." Valerie gritted the words out. She wanted to be rid of this half-fawning, half-authoritarian person, but she wanted the relief the sedative would bring more than bidding the woman to be gone. She sighed as the needle slid into her arm.

"That's all," said the nurse, "unless the doctor orders something more. It should get you through until he makes his morning rounds." The voice faded away along with the woman's footsteps.

Hospitals dispense drowsiness, but there is always someone to interrupt the natural tendencies of the body to heal through sleep. At six-thirty, a male aide arrived to feed her breakfast.

Why bother, Valerie wondered. It's just juice and gruel.

"There now, didn't we enjoy that?"

Dear God, thought Valerie, do they all talk alike?

At seven thirty, someone was there to take her temperature and blood pressure again. He was a skinny, young male nurse that patted her good shoulder. She had just started to drift into sleep again when the doctor and his assistant arrived.

The doctor's face was large and pink with medium eyebrows covering brown eyes. "You're doing fine," he assured her as he scanned her chart.

To his assistant, however, the doctor gave the vital information she wanted. "She has a broken arm and broken collarbone. We had to use titanium pins." His words were almost too rapid to follow. "She also has a concussion and lacerations of the face. Only a couple of the stitches are showing. She's lucky as plastic surgery won't be necessary. An accident like that can completely mutilate the face."

He leaned towards Valerie, close enough that she could see the pores in his face. "We've contacted your family. Someone will be in Seattle this week. When you're feeling better, we'll discuss what I've found." The doctor sounded pleased with himself and he too patted her on the good shoulder before he left with the heavy buttocks of his assistant trailing in his wake.

Valerie was stunned. What did he mean saying that someone from her family would be here? Insane! They wanted nothing to do with her. Which one would fly all the way from Des Moines, Iowa? Surely it would not be her parents who paid a substantial amount for her to stay away. That left Thomas, her younger, successful, and oh, so adored, younger brother. Would he leave his accounting firm for her, the outcast, over a broken bone or two? And what did the man mean about discussing what else he found?

She shriveled under the bedding. God, did they know? Would they report her? Would she need to find another place, secluded by day, yet close to a free-swinging community? There was always Los Angeles, but that was (in her eyes) too hot and sunshine bright. San Francisco for all of its decadence was like her parents. She was not wanted. Valerie's mind zigzagged back to her home. I wondered what happened to Robert when I wasn't there to meet him.

The hospital routine continued despite Valerie's horror of confinement. She was grateful for the painkillers and the blood they continued to give her. Gradually the pain subsided to a bearable level and day no longer blended into night. She surprised herself by sleeping the dark hours away, awakening at the entrance of the morning nurse, and feeling refreshed. As usual the man was full of plastic, good cheer.

"Well, look at you! Almost all of the needles are gone. Don't we feel much better today? By the end of the week, I'll bet most of the swelling will be gone and the bruises won't be so noticeable."

Valerie forced a smile to her face. It was obvious she couldn't fend for herself, yet she hated this dependency on others; she who had fought so desperately for her independence and the right to live as she wanted in accordance with her system's need. She noted the metal stand and tubing for the transfusions was still by her bed. Somehow the sustained transfusions held the key to the abatement of her usual physical demands.

A young resident doctor appeared. "Your assigned doctor is on an emergency. You're doing well. The transfusions will continue until your condition stabilizes." He did not say what her condition was.

Valerie was left to wonder. She hadn't needed that much blood when they were treating her for anemia so many years ago. The number of transfusions left her perplexed, but she made no demands on the staff, preferring the isolation and the bed rest. Several times she considered calling Robert, but refrained. There were others to consider also. What if they made new arrangements? Would she have to start all over again? She almost shrugged, but the pain in her shoulder made that impossible.

"Well, don't you look good!" Thomas, her brother, was standing in the doorway, his wide shoulders filling the open space, his ruddy face with its black, neatly trimmed beard, and his smile revealing the gleaming, white teeth with large spaces. His brown eyes were warm, tentatively friendly, and seemed to be begging for reconciliation. "May I come in?"

Valerie nodded, too stunned to argue. Thomas, grey, three-piece suited Thomas, was standing there smiling at her like she part of the family. A large bouquet was in his hand.

"You look well," she managed to say, but then Thomas always looked well. He jogged. He had his hair styled and his suits were always impeccable. Wool in winter and light wool in summer. He was the walking declaration of the young, successful, urban businessman.

Thomas behaved as though there had been no rupture in the family and set the bouquet in its elegant vase on her table. "These are from our parents. They wanted to come, but their cruise was scheduled months ago and they weren't able to get a refund." He gave a rueful smile at their parent's economic ways and continued. "Now wouldn't some light be better in this dreary place?"

"No!"

Thomas ignored her outburst and pulled the drapes open with a sweeping motion. "Of course, with all the clouds out there it doesn't make much difference. You can't imagine how much warmer it is…" He stopped speaking to stare at the sight of her hiding under the covers.

"Didn't they tell you, Valda? That's all over now." He stepped closer, gently untangled her hand, and pulled the covers away. "See, there's no pain now."

She stared at him and turned toward the window. It was true. The sharp, aching burn did not start. She sank back against the pillow. "Thomas, what is happening?"

"Valda, I don't have all of the medical terms, but it appears your condition is medical, not depravity. They won't be able to cure you, but like hemophilia it can be controlled. That is the basis of what Mama told me when she issued orders that I was to come here instead of them."

"You haven't spoken to the doctor?"

"No, Mama did. Fortunately, it wasn't Papa who answered the telephone or he would have hung up before the doctor could explain. She at least gave Dr. Hemlock..."

"Dr. Heinlein," Valerie corrected him.

Thomas waved the name away. "At any rate, she did listen. They're willing to pay for everything and want you to come home as soon as you are able. They sent me to proffer the olive branch in the way of flowers." He motioned to the gaudy colors in the vase.

Valerie clutched the covers, breathing deeply. It was too much. What did she have? Aloud she asked, "Is this contagious? Is it hereditary?"

"I don't know." Thomas dropped into the visitor's chair as he spoke. "That's one of the reasons I'm here. Kelly and I are being married this spring. I, we, need to know if it is genetic and, of course, we all want you to know that we understand now."

"When do you see the doctor again?" Thomas slipped easily into another subject.

"He usually stops by in the morning before his office hours." Her voice was low and dull. "I have no idea where he's located."

"Not a problem. I can find out. I'll check with the nurse's station before I leave. By the way, how long will that cast be on?"

"I've no idea. Really, Thomas, this is overwhelming. I'm exhausted." She closed her unbandaged eye. She wanted him to leave. The enormity of everything he said was beyond her comprehension. Did she want to change her ways? She liked her power.

She forced herself to speak pleasantly. "Do you want to stay at my place? I can give you the keys and the directions?"

"No, that's not necessary," he assured her. "The travel agency arranged everything with my secretary, including the lodging. There are taxis to whisk me around and I want to see something of Seattle as long as I'm here."

He stood and smiled at her. "I'll go now and let you rest. I can be back this evening or tomorrow morning when the doctor is here if that is preferable."

"Yes, tomorrow. Remember, he's here about seven-forty a.m." She opened her eye and shuddered at the open window. "Thomas, before you go, please, draw the drapes."

At his look of astonishment, she spoke lightly. "Old habits die hard, you know."

She made her mind blank; refusing to think, grateful that the afternoon nurse reattached the transfusion line. The blood warmed her and she drifted off into sleep.

It was not until evening that her mind began to function and then only because Robert called. Perhaps it was the hour he called. Seven thirty was her normal evening waking hour and the stupor left her as the telephone rang. Please, not Thomas, she thought as she answered, "Hello."

"Valerie, how are you? They said I could talk with you now, or visit, but you know how I detest hospitals."

"Robert, darling! How did you know I was here?" Pleasure turned her voice into a purr while excitement lurched within her.

"Who do you think called the medics? I wasn't but a few minutes behind you. I gave them what information I could and followed the ambulance to the hospital, but they said you wouldn't come around for a day or more, especially with that head injury. Are you, ah, going to be all right without me?"

"Yes, darling, I'll be fine. Nothing serious was shattered, but my head, arm, and collarbone will take some time to mend."

There was silence on the other end and she continued. "Naturally, I appreciate what you did. You will be the first one I call when I am released."

He chuckled then, his own pleasure rippling through the sound. She could see him, blood flushing over his pink cheeks, rising as high as the brow devoid of hair. That was one of the nice things about Robert. His blood was so close to the skin.

"Do you need anything? Are your funds sufficient?" he asked.

"No, I don't need a thing, but thank you. As usual, my parents are paying for everything." Even the blood, she thought.

"Well, you take care then. I'll send some flowers. I just don't wish to go into a hospital. You do understand?" He paused.

Yes, she did understand. He was terrified that someone would see the neck marks or detect his dependency on her. "Of course, I understand," she answered. "You will come when I call, won't you?" She needed his reassurance, not only his, but all of the others.

Would absence enable them to reject her? But there were always others. Seattle streets had its quota of wandering youths and there were always the gullible Goths. She preferred young males. Their blood was stronger. While it was sometimes necessary to pay for the first date, they gladly gave to her whenever she called, and they could be so very, very profitable. Her breath came in rapid pants as she thought of their physical contact.

Robert's voice broke through her reverie. Longing made his voice thick and unsteady. "Yes, yes, I'll be waiting for you."

She heard the click as he hung up and she returned the telephone to its cradle and drew in a deep breath. His call had invigorated her, and strangely, relaxed her. Now she could let her mind work again.

Controlled, not cured were the doctor's words to her mother. She, then to her family, would no longer be considered depraved, just diseased. Aunt Catryn would never have changed her mind. Aunt Catryn had proclaimed Valerie's nocturnal wanderings and unnatural skin tones were a warning sign.

The day Aunt Catryn turned the laundry management over to Valerie's parents, she watched Valerie every minute. Aunt Catryn would hang garlic wreaths around Valerie's neck.

Valerie remembered throwing the offensive thing away every day when going to school and every afternoon Aunt Catryn would replace it, threatening a spanking if she dared remove it. Then she would push Valerie out the door to play with the neighborhood children. The children promptly circled her chanting, "Valda stinks! Valda stinks!"

Valerie still couldn't decide which caused the most agony. Was it the sun searing into her skin or the taunts of the children?

A neighbor had told her mother how offensive the garlic was and Aunt Catryn had to desist making Valerie wear the necklace in public. Aunt Catryn's remarks about her skin and abnormal wide spaces between the teeth continued as long as she lived. Which was far too long, thought Valerie.

Valerie also remembered the struggle to rise in the morning. Sometimes Mama would drag her from the warm bed, but usually it was Aunt Catryn. School had been a blur as she sat stupefied, not really hearing or participating. She was always the one bullied on the playground. She would flee from the school as soon as possible, gratefully closing the front door behind her. She tried not to emerge until evening, or until pushed out the next morning.

Nights she would roam the silent house, content with the quiet and her fantasies. Hunger would strike her then and she would raid the refrigerator or the cookie jar, but nothing, nothing ever satisfied her. One evening she picked up the tray of meat being defrosted for the next day's meal. She answered some deep, agonizing desire and lifting the foam tray to her mouth, she began drinking the blood pooled on the bottom.

It was filling, oh so filling, and the taste left her panting for more. She squeezed the meat, letting the blood drain down inside her mouth and in her mind came the words, "but human blood is better, much better."

She licked the remaining traces of blood from her fingers. She knew she would need more and took a roast from the freezer and hid it in her room. The next evening she took a chicken. Each thawed piece was meticulously rewrapped and replaced in the freezer. She began keeping her room in perfect order. No one would have any reason to enter. Of course, she was discovered. Aunt Catryn, always suspicious, ransacked her room after discovering blood on one of her sheets.

It was a frightful scene with Aunt Catryn making the sign of the cross and wailing, "I should never have left you alone with Grandfather Vladimir. You had blood on your mouth when I returned. He contaminated you! I know it! A curse upon him and a curse upon you!"

She could still hear Papa shouting in the background about how she had always been an unnatural child. Mama and Aunt Catryn had collapsed upon each other wailing and moaning that they were undone.

To protect themselves, the family hung garlic over the doors and windows. Aunt Catryn wove a cross of the vile bulb and hung it above Valerie's bed. Only then had she been permitted to sleep in her bed again. A priest was called for consultation.

The priest came. He was a young man who listened patiently and his eyes filled with compassion when he looked at her, a skinny, undersized child with thin, dark hair. He refused to do an exorcism, explaining that he had no authority to do so. The procedure itself was long and involved, and required permission from the Cardinal. He suggested the child needed a doctor as urgently as they all needed spiritual counseling. She had adored him and wanted to hug this surprise ally, but Mama had wedged her securely between herself and Papa.

To placate the priest, they'd taken her to a doctor. "She has anemia," he informed them. A series of off-again-on-again transfusions and Vitamin B-12 shots were started. A year later when Valda turned thirteen, the doctor had a new pronouncement. "She doesn't have anemia. She is not responding to treatment. There is an imbalance in her system. I suggest you take her to the University of Iowa Hospital for more tests."

Papa, of course, refused. "It would be a waste of good money just like the treatments I have paid for all year." By then he had turned Aunt Catryn's laundry into a chain of dry cleaning establishments and was still expanding. He had no time for any other travel and could not spare his wife.

Her early teenage years were a nightmare. Her body refused to grow or change. She would spend days in bed, too weak to rise for food. Then she would be compelled to begin her nightly prowling, sometimes snitching bloody meat from the fridge and other times sneaking money from her mother's purse and splurging at the all night supermarket. Usually she bought liver. That was always bloody.

At her mother's insistence, tutors were hired for her. Most were hefty blondes. All came at night when she was awake and Valda would wonder how their blood would taste. Even when the tutors were female, Valda wondered about their blood. Somehow she knew that for her, male would be better—much better.

During her fifteenth year, she began to change. There was a slight thickening in the chest and hips. Her face remained an unnatural red, the teeth wide-spaced, and her hair so thin she needed a hairpiece. Her hair had never grown long enough to touch her shoulders and it remained a pathetic, dull black. Her father, as always, ignored her. Her mother had given up hope for her ever changing and became inattentive. Her mother became pregnant again. Aunt Catryn grew older and frailer as she neared ninety and continued to make the sign of the cross every time she entered a room occupied by Valda.

Valda hated her. She blamed Aunt Catryn for all the misery and misfortune in her life.

As her sixteenth birthday neared, her tutor was more her own age and he too was skinny. He was incredibly shy with girls, even more incredible he was shy around her. He needed money to attend college and worked in one of her father's stores in the afternoon and then taught her in the evening. At first Danny would avert his face instead of looking directly at her, shifting his blue eyes towards the ceiling or using them to study the table. He began to realized that she was not desirable, not one of the popular girls. She could not be a threat and they became friends.

Aunt Catryn would retire early. Sometimes her parents had business or social engagements and the young would be left alone, studying in the library. None of her family was there for her sixteenth birthday. She began to weep bitterly. Danny put his arms around her to comfort her. Only his arms had not remained around her shoulders. They slipped down and his fingers unbuttoned her skirt. He ran his hands over her thin buttocks and began swaying her body against his, the manhood part of him hard against her belly. His gift was her only present that night.

He did not realize the power of his gift. When the pain of the final penetration hit her, she retaliated by clamping her teeth into his neck and shoulder. Her passion assuaged, she became contrite and began to lick the blood away from the tooth-marked skin while making soothing sounds in her throat. That had been the best part, the blood, warm and salty, and, oh, how rich!

She slept soundly and awakened at seven o'clock the next evening full of life and exuberance. Now she knew what her body craved and what it needed. She knew she could exist in this world, but first she must be stronger.

After her lessons, she and Danny began taking long walks in the soft, Indian summer nights. Instead of stopping at the supermarket, they would go to one of her father's dry cleaning outlets and make love. At the climax she would bite him and lap away the blood. It was a slow deterioration, but his hours, work, study, and loss of blood began to sap his strength. Although he was young, he became less nourishing. Valda knew she would soon need a replacement or Danny would suffer too much. Night school would be the answer.

There she could select from many others to fulfill her needs and she would please her parents by graduating from high school. Her own apartment would be a necessity. For like her grandfather, she shunned the day.

Her father refused in cold, authoritarian tones. "You are needed at home when your Mama delivers our son. He will enhance our name, not besmirch it as you do."

Besmirch was it? Valda plotted. The solution was simple and Danny obediently helped. He brought a friend along one night as she had ordered. Ted was a handsome, broad shouldered hunk and very willing to prove his manhood.

She proved Ted's manhood over and over again that night while biting and licking, biting and licking each time. Aunt Catryn came into the den once and scuttled back to her room.

The young men left shortly before her parents returned.

Her father was outraged to find her still awake and the CD player blasting into the night. "Why aren't you in bed?"

"Why should I be in bed, Papa? I am awake and alive." She smiled and whirled to the music.

Her mother stared at her, the weariness from the day's labor and evening's meeting etched in her brown eyes. "Why, Valda, my little one, you, you look so good."

For once her Father actually looked at her and opened his eyes to see the rosy, pink color on her cheeks, the deep red of her lips, the new gloss to her black hair, and black eyes that snapped with life and vitality. They had stared at her with opened mouths. Their daughter was a normal looking teenager, not a beauty, but one that did not have to be hidden away in shame.

Aunt Catryn appeared at the door to the room holding a cross in front of her. Pointing it at Valda, she intoned, "She is one of our evil ones. I want her out! Tonight she had two men with her and she drank their blood."

The old woman leaned against the door, crooning through toothless gums. "Evil, evil, she is evil. God forgive me, I am the one who named her and left her with my grandfather." She backed down the hall still clutching the cross; her old voice becoming a scream. "Get her out of here, or tomorrow I change my will!"

It was the first time Valda realized the man she called grandfather was Aunt Catryn's grandfather and she stored the information to dwell on later as her father was questioning her.

"What in God's name was that about?"

"That, Papa, means that I had two young men over tonight and we all satisfied each other."

Her father's face became a blotched pattern of varying shades of red patches. The heavy brows skimmed toward his hairline. He might have beaten her, but he dared not let loose of Mama who was sagging against him, unable to bear the weight of this revelation and that of the coming child. He helped Mama to the sofa and turned to Valda. "Explain," he snapped through full, parted lips, almost snarling the word.

"I gave them what they wanted, and I, Papa, I lapped their blood. See how strong it has made me." She raised her arms and twirled around. It was true. She was stronger than both of them. Through the force of her will she was bending their will to hers. Mama was groaning, her hands over her ears.

"It seems Aunt Catryn has been right about me, but garlic and crosses don't really matter." She repeated the words from long ago. "They are the myth part."

"I'll have you locked up like the mad person you are!"

"No, Janos, no." Mama was crying now. "Not my little one, not my baby girl."

"Little one? The little one to worry about is the one you carry now."

"Janos, think. We would have to explain to friends, to associates. You see, I am thinking about this one now." She laid her hand on the huge area protruding above her lap. "Soon he will come. He must not be teased about a mad sister. Let her go."

She turned to Valda and asked, "Do you promise to finish high school?"

"Of course, Mama, and I'll finish college too. It can all be done at night. All I need is my own apartment and no one will ever know about any of you."

Her father stood between them, his stocky body rigid as he clenched and unclenched his fists. "Do you realize how much it will cost?"

"Cost?" asked her mother. "Who cares? There will be peace in this household. Peace for me, for Aunt Catryn, for you, for the little one, and, dear God, I pray there will be peace for you too, Valda."

And so it was accomplished. When she turned the key in the door to her own place, she knew she was free. Free of all of them and she could go to bed when the sun rose and pick and choose among those who would support her. She never charged her current favorites, but after high school, the cost of college hardened her outlook and she took their money to supplement her income. The ones she chose were all like Danny. One time with her and they met her demands for blood. She kept in touch with her mother and was pleased when the son they wanted was born. Yet, she experienced bitterness when she realized that this child was everything to them that she had not been.

The pictures of him would make her wonder. He had the same round, ruddy face and the same wide spaces between his teeth. While he was a heavier, stockier child, his hair was coarse and black. According to her mother, this one also had a tendency to sleep late and prowl the house at night. Since Grandfather Trepas (how ancient had he been, Valerie wondered) no longer visited them, there were no neck wounds on Thomas. The family could accept the son's nighttime activities. "Oh, he's just a night owl," was how they phrased it.

* * *

Thomas arrived early enough to share a cup of coffee during breakfast. He was full of gossip about Des Moines, awed at the steep hills of Seattle, and obviously would prefer talking with anyone but her. She noted with amusement the gray in his hair, the lines at the corners of his eyes, the gentle sagging of the jowls hidden by his beard, while she, sixteen years his senior, had none of those aging signs. She too was interested in what the doctor would say for during the night they had taken the transfusion apparatus away. Her lifeline was gone and panic was beginning to build.

Doctor Heinlein came charging into the room at eight o'clock, a dark suit covering his short, lean body, and as always he looked freshly barbered and shaved. His heavy, rumpled assistant was still trailing in his wake, beads of sweat forming on his forehead from the exertion of following pure, electric energy.

"Tomorrow you'll have an X-ray and the facial bandages can be removed. I've set up an examination with the orthopedic surgeon. If no more operations are necessary, you'll be out of here in two days. You can go home; however, I prefer that you rent an apartment near here for weekly physicals and the possibility that you will need outpatient care." His speech was like the man's movements, a rapid flow of words to make up for the too few hours allotted to accomplish a day's work.

"Instead of transfusions, I've ordered injections of heme, that's short for hematin, every twenty-four hours. We'll continue to monitor your blood to determine how the dosage works or if we need to make an adjustment in the dosage."

He turned to Thomas. "You might want to make an appointment to have your own blood tested."

His pronouncements had not enlightened them and sister and brother stared at him with a blank glaze in their eyes. Dr. Heinlein grinned. "Now, you and your brother would like to know what I've discovered, right?"

Without waiting for a reply, he continued. "We've known about porphyria, a defect which produces prophyrins in excess, for some years. Ongoing research at the University of British Columbia, however, has shown that the lack of just one enzyme can block the production porphyrin. Porphyrin is needed to modify iron so it won't oxidize, rust if you will. The worst condition causes extreme body hairiness, deformities of the body, and pulls the lips and gums back from the teeth. People with the worst cases do not live very long. Yours is obviously controllable. Drinking blood is useless, but heme and intravenous glucose injections are working. I also recommend high glucose drinks. You've noticed your sensitivity to light has diminished."

Valerie nodded.

"What causes it?" asked Thomas.

"Usually the cause is a faulty gene. Would either of you know if your family intermarried sometime in the recent past?"

Valerie laughed. "Our parents are second cousins. Both of their parents were first cousins. It's a Hungarian-Transylvanian family tradition of arranged marriages."

Dr. Heinlein nodded. "I thought so."

"Do you mean I can pass this trait on to any children that Kelly and I might have?"

"There is always that possibility, but a geneticist will be able to answer your question."

"Why does the sunlight hurt?" Valerie had to know.

"The prophyrins excite oxygen atoms. The oxygen becomes an active form affecting living cells, particularly those stored under the skin, along the bones, and causes cellular destruction. In a sensitive area, it causes pain. You probably learned very early to stay inside."

"Except when it was cloudy," said Valerie. "That is why this area is such a great place to live."

The doctor smiled. "A wise choice, however, once we have the correct dosage, you can live anywhere you please. We'll see you tomorrow."

After they left, Thomas cleared his throat. "Well, it looks like I need to get back to Des Moines, and Kelly and I will need to see a geneticist."

"I doubt if they will know what you are asking." Scorn lay thick and heavy in her voice. "They'll probably hang garlic around your neck as a safeguard."

"Really, Valda, we aren't that backward."

"Didn't you hear him? Ongoing research is a term for 'we're using you as a guinea pig to test the hypothesis.' That's the reason he wants to keep such a close watch on my symptoms."

"Perhaps," Thomas conceded. "My reservations are for this afternoon and I will have to leave." He paused as though waiting for a comment, and then asked, "When shall I tell Mama to expect you home?"

Valerie considered. "There are still weeks of therapy ahead and there are things I need to think through."

"For God's sake, she's seventy-nine! Papa is even older. They've supported you all these years. I should know. I've written the checks for the last fifteen."

Valerie looked at her brother. He was so like her Aunt Catyn and father. Control the money, and you control the recipient. "What am I supposed to do when I return home? Stay locked in my room again?"

"You could work at the office. It wouldn't take long to get the hang of the simpler tasks. You can't go on living off your parents all of your life waiting for a larger share when they die."

She laughed. Did they really thing that their meager checks were her only source of income?

"Thomas, Papa wrote me out of their will years ago. Accepting their monthly stipend is the only way I'll collect any of the inheritance. Be reasonable. I can't go anywhere for at least two months. Go home now and I promise to write to Mama," she paused, "and Papa."

Strangers all of their lives, they could only stare at each other. Thomas turned and left without saying good bye and quiet filled the room. Yes, she did have much to think about and to consider. Could she really live a life in the daylight? It might be an illusion of life for she would grow older and older. The gift from her grandfather's bite kept her young in face and body, but life in the sunlight might mean that she could have children. She wondered if sand between the toes would feel better when warmed by the sun. Would blood taste any different?

It was six weeks before the physical therapist released her and two months before Dr. Heinlein thought she could return home. The daily injections of heme needed to continue, but the routine of daily testing was discontinued. Monthly checkups should suffice unless she noticed a change. It had been two months of considering all the aspects of her new life. When she was released from the hospital, she felt like a butterfly free to soar in the sun; except, butterflies are beautiful and delicate, and live but one month. Was she still Valerie? How long would she live?

She was the one who had rejected outward family traditions while becoming the embodiment of the family's hidden heritage. She began to spend hours on the waterfront watching the gulls swirl over Puget Sound or float on the water. She smelled the great, busy, pushed-together-crowd of humans that appeared during the daylight hours and who ignored her. Each day she would examine her features in the mirror, wondering what changes the injected glucose, heme, and outside sun would inflict. The day she discovered a gray hair, she viciously yanked it out with tweezers. When she found crow's feet forming at the corners of her eyes, she bought a larger pair of sunglasses and wore them continuously, day or night, and always, always, she was hungry.

She remembered crying for food long ago. Aunt Catryn was watching her, but the loud knocking on the door had summoned Aunt Catryn to the hospital. Valerie could not remember who had been injured. She could remember her aunt rushing through the room while struggling into a coat and screaming at the old man sitting in the chair not to hurt the child. Aunt Catryn's screaming had frightened her and she crawled up onto the old man's lap. He snuggled her against him and began crooning in the language that Mama and Papa used at Christmas time. When she awoke, she was hungry and started to cry.

"Yes, that is true," came the old voice. "Hunger drives us all." She felt his breath on her neck and then it felt like pin pricks, only warmer and then he held her against his neck. "Bite and drink, little one, and be full for you will need this."

Valerie did not remember how long they were together. She remembered him telling her, "You will always remember this time with me. Most of the things they will tell you later will not be true. What I have given you is a gift of love and a gift of power. You will find blood in many places, but human blood is better, much, much better."

Valerie smiled as she remembered the ancient one and stood. She was his legacy and she had to continue the family tradition. Someday she would select the next one.

* * *

It was good, so good to be home again. Valerie rocked with bare feet on the lush carpet and touched the teak furniture, the crystal vases, the stone and wood sculptures set in every room. The checks from her parents had not purchased these items. The beautiful articles had been paid for by her faithful clients. She stroked the soft velvet of the maroon drapes and then pulled them back to look upward at the moon floating over Mount Si.

She heard Robert stirring in the bed behind her, his scarred, nude body outlined in the dim light. The new openings on his neck and shoulders were flecked with blood, the smell exciting her senses.

"Aren't you coming back, Valerie?" he mumbled. His tone was weary, but the needing for her was in his plaintive, almost pleading question.

"Valda, darling, Valda, it's an old family name.

Old Things

The 1890's house had been built on a secluded hill of the Pacific Northwest. It was the long ago home of a minor timber baron who preferred isolation. Decades later the area around the hill sprouted houses instead of hemlocks and cedars. The baron and then his wife passed away and the house became the abode of rats, an occasional opossum, and bats.

"It looks so lonely," Chrissie exclaimed to Pat on one of their rare afternoon walks.

Pat adjusted his sunglasses and looked at the house.

"The outside does have a certain Victorian charm, but the rooms were usually quite small."

"Yes, it would need remodeling, but it won't hurt to call the realtor on that sign. It looks like it's been there forever. If the price is low enough, we can have the space we want in the area we want." She smiled at Pat, loving that frown that creased his lean face whenever he was thinking.

"It would be time consuming."

Chrissie almost stamped her foot. "Everything in life is time consuming. We both work long hours and bring home an adequate income. Remember, the CPA said we should have a mortgage for the interest deduction. This way we will have all the room we want with our own offices and a real media room. Most of all, Pat, I want my own space where I can put up things and take them down without consulting a landlord."

"We don't have any paper to write down the telephone number."

"Really, Pat, one of us should be able to remember Rose of Shannon Realty. I'll bet the big boys wouldn't even bother with this property."

Her guess had proven correct. The original estate had set the price too high. The will stipulated that the house never be torn down. Gradually, the heirs moved, grew older, and died. The property languished in some forgotten file. The building boom had passed it by when people discovered how much it cost to lift a house, reinforce the existing foundation, and then during the restoration tear out walls to create a living space for twenty-first century living. They purchased it with favorable terms and at a much lower price than the listing.

Chrissie took to snapping pictures of every phase from bulldozing out the blackberry brambles, thimbleberry bushes, rotted stumps sprouting huckleberries, and ferns blocking access to the house. She tried desperately to save some of the old wild rhododendrons, and ancient red cedars, but Pat objected.

"Chrissie, we'll have a landscaper put in the new hybrids. Their flowers are much larger. We need smaller trees around the house to let in light. Those can be sold for lumber and help pay for the landscaping."

His practicality infringed on her sense of ecological history, but she acquiesced. On one of their forays to record progress, they had a visitor.

A young man from next door sauntered over to survey the work.

"Did you buy the haunted house?"

"Is it haunted? Have you seen a ghost?" Both Chrissie and Pat spoke at the same time.

He laughed. "No, not me, and neither has anyone else. Children just manage to scare themselves on Halloween. My Great-aunt said the Native Americans insisted this was ground to be avoided or people who visited should leave fish and deer offerings to insure their children would live. She also insisted that something gurgled down below, but that was probably just water after one of our wet years. Lately, the brush has been too thick to get into the house. I hope you get all the rats and other creatures that have taken up residency there."

"What about the Native Americans? Do they come back?"

"Naw, the feds dispersed them over one hundred years ago. Our state doesn't bother showcasing the Indian culture like Arizona or New Mexico." He ambled off.

It had taken almost fourteen months, but now the home was rebuilt. The call from the contractor confirmed it. Chrissie called Pat.

"The renovation is finished!" Excitement bubbled in Chrissie's voice. "They'll do the Certificate of Occupation (C of O) inspection on Monday. Our contractor will call the minute he is informed. Once it clears, we'll be able to move within the week."

"Excellent, I'll be home at six. Shall we celebrate tonight or wait for the C of O results?"

Chrissie ran her left hand through her straight brown hair. "Let's wait until everything is cleared. Who knew that old house would take so long?" She smiled remembering the day they saw it. Both had worn their walking shoes and outfits. She had deliberately coordinated the clothes to show off their height and slender frames. It was something she did: decorate for moods, for events, and now she had a four thousand, five hundred square foot home to decorate.

The old house had been painted cream with brown trim to fit the city's guidelines. Blakely, the middle-aged City Inspector, admired the sweep of the roof and the clean lines of the porch when he stepped out of the city vehicle. He walked briskly to the front, inserted the master key into the lockset, walked into the house, and closed the door.

Newsome, the contractor, arrived forty-five minutes later. He got out of his pickup and went to the front door. He felt there had been enough time for the inspection and wondered why the city vehicle was still there.

At the door, Newsome used his master key and let himself in. "Hallo," he shouted and his voice echoed back to him. Strange the house felt and sounded empty. Newsome glanced around and began walking through the house when he heard a faint banging noise. As he neared the kitchen, the banging grew louder. In the kitchen, he realized the sound came from the basement door.

"What's wrong?" he yelled.

"The door is locked"

Newsome turned the knob, used his master key again, and yanked on the door. Nothing happened. "Hold on something's wrong."

"Hurry up. I've got another appointment." The man was screaming.

Newsome tried again and pulled harder. The door inched open as if some force were holding it back. The inspector rushed out, his face mottled white and red, and breathing rapidly.

"Get that door fixed and check out that sump pump again. Then we'll see about a C of O." He stormed out of the house.

Newsome placed his call to the Bensons.

"Sorry, folks, there seems to be something wrong with the basement door. It'll be a week, before I can send the crew back."

Chrissie decided to break out the wine bottle anyway. What was one week after waiting for fourteen months?

Once again the empty house beckoned to those without a place to sleep. This time it was a two legged animal in a scruffy hoodie fleeing a downpour. He smashed a back window and entered the house. The carpet was soft and inviting. Morning brought more rain, and he dug a protein bar out of his backpack.

Tom munched away and decided he might as well check this place out. Nothing else to do until the rain let up. The kitchen was bare and he decided to try the basement in the hopes that a place this large would have a well-stocked wine cellar. Instead, he found a small room waiting to be filled with bottles. He shrugged and checked out the rest of the space. Surely, someone left something, anything that he would be able to sell. As he approached the sump pump, he heard a strange gurgling noise. What was it?

It seemed to be guttural, yet somehow metallic. As he neared the low spot for the drain to empty out any water that might enter, he felt a pulling sensation. Some primeval instinct warned him to turn, drop, to his knees, and scrabble away from the sound. He fought his way to the top of stairs, and tried to open the door. It wouldn't budge. Tom began banging on the door, screaming, ramming his skinny shoulders into the solid wooden door. Why in the hell hadn't these people used a hollow core door? Sobs began to shake his body, and his voice grew hoarse as the force drawing him backwards grew stronger and the gurgling sound became a roar filling the spaces and his head.

Tom felt himself being drawn backward and his feet slipped out from beneath him. His consciousness fled. He came to as his feet neared the drain. He was gasping for air; thankful the drain had a metal grate over it. He tried to roll away from the force pulling his body. Somehow the grate had swung upward. He tried to force his body to roll, and then grasped desperately at the cement, but there was nothing to hold onto. He screamed as his feet and legs slipped into the yawning drain. Huge hands grasped his knees and yanked.

From below a slurping sound would have been heard if anyone was there to hear. The grate slammed down and quiet descended over the basement.

* * *

Newsome walked through the house to check every door and window before calling the city for another inspection. "Wonder why they left their backpack," he said to the walls and removed the scuffed up, smelly bag. It took two days to repair the window.

"This is ridiculous!" Chrissie was on the verge of screaming. "We want to move in!"

"Don't worry Mrs. Benson. I'll be right there and call you when the inspection is over."

This time, Newsome followed the inspector throughout the house and basement. He waited until six p.m. before calling the Benson's.

"Great news Mrs. Benson, the house is ready for you."

Chrissie danced around the room.

"Break out the champagne, Pat! We're homeowners!"

One week later, Chrissie was sitting cross-legged on the basement floor sorting through piles of paintings they had acquired over the years. She chose four to take upstairs for the living room. The wine cellar needed a vivid painting to set the mood. She held up one and eyed it critically. She was distracted by a gurgling noise.

How strange. Is there something wrong with the electrical? She walked around the basement trying to find the source. She finally stopped near the sump pump. Strange, it's not on, but maybe I should call Newsome and have a man sent out. Before she could move a force gripped at her legs and shoulders and her eyes grew wide as the grate over the drain swung upward.

Sheer instinct made her whirl and start to run. Only this wasn't running. It was slowly lifting one foot and setting it down and then the next. She leaned forward to give momentum to each agonizing step. She grabbed at a chair and tried to force it behind her. The force wrenched the chair towards the hole while the humming grew louder. She released her hands and landed on the cement covered tile floor. Pain shot through her back and legs and she struggled to regain her feet. The chair slid into the empty, gurgling hole. A howl came from below. The force pulling at her seemed to double and she screamed

* * *

Pat returned from the store with the wine bottles for the cellar. "Chrissie, I'm back," he announced. When no answer came, he searched the house. There was nothing, No note, no message on the computer, nothing. Her purse was still in her closet, and the house was empty.

Two hours later he called the police. They would not let him file a missing person report until morning. Within two days, he was a person of interest. Within a month they arrested him, but nothing was ever proven in a court of law. Pat became a bitter man living out his days in an empty house that gurgled during a storm.

The Human Condition

At first glance, this Saturday morning was not unlike any other summer day in western Washington. True, the weather was balmier than normal and no rain was falling. Yet, something was wrong. The Baxter's sprawled in their side-by-side lawn lounges that were setting in thick, green grass bordered by flower beds and rhododendrons. There was no low murmur of voices and no movement from the two pajama clad people looking upward into the morning sun.

Very little in Darlene Kimball's fifty plus years had prepared her for the scene she found in the Baxter's yard that morning. She'd entered by the side gate that separated their property and advanced full stride toward the chairs, only to stop abruptly. At first she wasn't sure that her eyes were focusing. She couldn't possibly be seeing all that dried blood. She put one pudgy hand on her throat and gasped, "Oh, my God! Where did all that blood come from?"

The Snoqualmie police are very efficient. They arrived with their sirens, ambulances, technicians, and equipment. They took pictures; they measured the bodies and the distance from the house, and refused to let anyone approach until they were finished. The inside of the house was dusted for prints, and carpet, hair, and blood samples were gathered for testing. Their responses to the reporters amounted to "no comment."

Detective Pat Williams felt there was nothing to say. He could not admit that a man and his wife had been murdered, and had nothing as a motive, not even robbery. The coroner had given a tentative "after midnight" for time of death. Williams started to wipe his face with the clean, pocket handkerchief his wife always provided, but changed his mind. Lately, she'd been spray starching everything. Why, he could not fathom, unless it was to irritate him. Other wives didn't even bother to iron handkerchiefs. It was nearly eleven o'clock, the weather unseasonably warm, and his feet were beginning to hurt. It was going to be a long day.

His blue eyes searched for his new partner and found him outside, "We'd better go next door. Maybe they heard something last night. Who knows, maybe we'll get lucky."

Young Don Adler followed his superior through the backyard to the front, his brown eyes taking in the expensive homes and meticulously landscaped yards. "This isn't exactly the place you'd expect to find your neighbors with their throats cut."

Adler was twenty-six, two inches over six feet, and precisely the type of military and college trained man the department had hoped to lure away from the metropolitan areas of Seattle and Bellevue. "I wonder why they moved the bodies outside after murdering them in bed," he finished.

"What makes you think it was they?"

"It was either they or a very strong one to move two bodies."

"Hmm, while you're wondering, figure out why nothing of value was taken." They walked up to a door with the sign, "Welcome to Kimball's Court."

"Someone didn't like the Baxter's." He answered while ringing the Kimball's doorbell.

Edward Kimball opened the door. He looked to be about sixty, a tall, portly man with iron grey hair and glasses. He was clearly annoyed by the polite request to question both him and his wife. "I suppose it is necessary," he grumbled as he led them into an overly decorated front room.

"Please have a chair. I'll get Mrs. Kimball."

Darlene Kimball was about fifty-four, tall, and like her husband, accustomed to eating well. Her dark hair was cut short and waved in front with frizzy curls over the rest of her head. She wore dark clothes to conceal the ever thickening body. Under ordinary circumstances, her face was pink and wrinkle free, but today it was blotched and puffy from crying.

Detective Williams introduced themselves and became reassuring. "We won't take long. We understand you found the Baxter's and called us."

"Yes." She nervously brushed the velvet on the chair arm.

"We wonder if you might have heard anything unusual last night, particularly any time after midnight."

"No," Darlene answered. "We're both heavy sleepers and the walls are well insulated." Her flat Midwestern twang cracked as her voice rose in pitch. "Last night? But they were outside."

Williams decided not to elucidate. "Could you tell us a little about the Baxter's? How long you've known them, and if they had visitors last night."

"Well, of course, we knew Bette before, but Walter only since we moved here. They're song writers and set designers for shows. You know, like in Las Vegas and those places. That's why this is horrible. I mean, with knowing Bette and her dear aunts for so many years."

Detective Williams leaned forward. Something in her tone interested him. "Are you saying you both knew Mrs. Baxter before you moved here? When and where was that?"

"Back home in Iowa. We graduated from high school the same year."

"Then you kept up your friendship all of these years?"

The Kimball's exchanged uneasy glances. "No, she answered. "You see, I grew up on a farm and Bette in town. She was always different from the rest of us. She liked short skirts and flashy jewelry and makeup. We were never really friends until recently. She left Brandon, that's where we went to high school, right after graduation. It nearly broke her aunts' hearts. They raised her you know."

"We didn't know Bette was our neighbor," Mrs. Kimball continued, "until after we moved in. I'd never approved of her past life, or all of her marriages, but it was nice to have someone from home to talk with. I didn't have to explain why I said or did things a certain way. Bette knew. That's why when the invitation for our fortieth reunion came in the mail this morning, I went right over to see if she had one too. She's been so nervous and irritable lately, a trip home would have given her a new perspective, possibly even brought her to her senses."

Detective Williams kept a straight face and stole a glance at Adler. The young man looked boggle-eyed at the rambling speech. Mrs. Kimball had managed to infer a great deal. "Why do you think Mrs. Baxter was so uneasy?

It was interesting to note the tight lines around Mr. Kimball's mouth.

"Well, Walter had gambled a great deal in Las Vegas. They worked the smaller shows, you know. At any rate, he lost thousands of dollars. Bette just couldn't take it. The telephone calls, you know."

"No, ma'am. What telephone calls?" Williams was almost ashamed of his phrasing.

"Why for the money, of course. Oh my goodness! Is that what happened? Somebody came after the money?" Mrs. Kimball stood.

"I'm sorry. I wish I had never left Brandon. People are decent there." She hurried from the room, sobbing.

Edward Kimball shifted uneasily. "Darlene finds it difficult to adjust to urban life styles. She's a bit prudish about behavior. Is there anything else?"

"Do you know anything about the gambling debts?"

"Only what Darlene said. I think she's exaggerated the pressure."

"Did the Baxter's have company last night? Did you or Mrs. Kimball see anyone there later in the evening?"

"No, we didn't notice anything. Is it possible to keep our names out of the papers? It's unsettling enough without publicity."

"Not really. It's still a free press." Williams looked at him. "Do you know why the Baxter's settled here and not Las Vegas or Reno?"

"Walter and Bette were tired of the constant nightlife. There aren't the same temptations here and this is Walter's hometown. They had their contracts, the internet, and they traveled a great deal. They planned to retire here eventually."

"Do you mind telling us what you do for a living?"

Kimball answered automatically. "I'm the head of a sales department for lumber and related products and based in Issaquah. Our territory includes Oregon and Idaho. Why?"

"I'm curious. Did you notice any strange cars parked outside or driving past the Baxter's?"

"No, not offhand and the streets are deliberately zoned to be too narrow for street parking. I'm not home much during the day, so I wouldn't know about street traffic."

"Thank you, Mr. Kimball. We'll be back when Mrs. Kimball feels better."

As they stepped outside, Williams noted the curious were still there. Some, less bold stood in their yards or peered out of windows. All denied hearing anything unusual during the evening. They checked with Officer Jensen, a stocky local man. "Did you find any weapons?"

Jensen shrugged. His face was pink from the unexpected sunshine. "No, sir, but this area's pockmarked with cul-de-sacs and green belts. Someone could have stuffed it under a log or thrown it in a blackberry thicket."

Williams nodded in agreement and they headed inside the Baxter home to make one last check on the bedroom. The halls were lined with good prints and celebrity photos. The bedroom had wide, plush scarlet drapes. The king-sized scarlet, velvet coverlet had slipped to the white carpet. Both were stained with blood. The murderer had stripped the sheets. Why? Why move the bodies? An empty wine bottle was on the floor, but there were no wine glasses.

"Did you get the glasses?"

The "Uh huh," was perfunctory. The empty bottle remained on the floor. "They were probably drunk when they went to bed. Have someone get that wine bottle."

The investigation became routine legwork: checking on friends, business associates, professional contacts, all listed neatly in the Baxter's appointment and address files. It kept them busy while waiting for the autopsy and DNA results.

The gambling losses were checked. Walter Baxter had lost heavily, but his wife's jewelry served as collateral and, unfortunately for theory, the debt was being repaid. Until his death, no one worried about the one thousand dollars due each month.

"Maybe they wanted to make an example of him," suggested Adler.

"In the backwoods of western Washington where nobody hears about it?" retorted Williams.

Their file on the Baxter's grew. It was two weeks later that the autopsy report arrived and Williams finally had something to question someone about. "She had just had an abortion," he chortled and made an appointment to see Dr. Travis at the Minor Medical Center in Seattle.

Dr. Travis was not happy to be questioned. He smoothed one surgically clean hand over thinning, brown hair, arranged his bland features in a disapproving frown, and respectively declined to answer. It took a graphic description of the death scene to loosen his tongue. Finally, he admitted Mrs. Baxter had an abortion two days before the murder.

"At her age, Mrs. Baxter had not wanted a child," Dr. Travis explained, then hesitated. "You have no idea as to who the killer is?"

Williams shook his head no.

The doctor drummed his fingers on the desk. "The child was probably fathered by someone other than Mr. Baxter."

Williams' eyebrows shot upward. "Why do you say that?"

"Mrs. Baxter had not told Mr. Baxter about the pregnancy or the true nature of her visits. She simply told him it was a change of life problem. It is my understanding that he had a vasectomy. Since he was never my patient, I can't verify that."

Williams left the doctor's office pleased and perplexed. He had another nugget of information, but which way did it lead? He put the thought out of his mind as he guided the car through the narrow, twisting lanes of the parking garage made for nothing but compact autos.

As the days drug by, they found themselves devoting less and less time to the Baxter's file. The Baxter residence was in the Snoqualmie Ridge development above the business section and old town of Snoqualmie. It was a bedroom community for Issaquah and Bellevue. On a chance, they began showing Mrs. Baxter's picture to the bars and restaurants in the nearby towns. Adler struck pay dirt in a small, trendy lounge in Fall City.

"Are you ready for a description of the guy with her?" Adler barely waited for Williams to nod. "He's about sixty, tall, iron grey hair, a portly gentleman that wears glasses."

"Kimball!" exploded Williams.

Adler grinned with satisfaction. "Do we pick him up, or do we have him come in for questioning?"

"Neither, right away. Find out where he works, his schedule, and let me know. Have someone check with the Cedar Hills and Cedar Falls landfills to see if anyone recognizes Kimball's description. You have one day."

It took Adler two days. They visited Kimball at his office in Issaquah. Mr. Kimball did not keep them waiting.

"I'm short of time, but this is for a neighbor. Please have a seat." He indicated the chairs set at the front of his desk.

The chairs were substantial, taking their weight with ease. The woodwork and ceiling moldings were impressive and the desk a shining sea of undisturbed teak.

Williams came right to the point. "You were a frequent escort of Mrs. Baxter. You'd meet at the Colonial Inn in Fall City and then leave before nine or ten o'clock in your own vehicles. We have proof that on other nights, you visited motels in Issaquah. Before you answer, you might want a lawyer present."

Kimball sat back, his face graying, his body and jowls sagging. "Darlene will never go with me. She won't even go to restaurants anymore." He removed his glasses and ran his hand over his face, before carefully replacing them. "Wally liked to write his songs at night and didn't want distractions. Yes, we would meet there, but it was never secretive. I just never mentioned it to Darlene."

"Did she just assume you were working late, or did you call her and tell her that?"

"I told Darlene I would be late." Kimball grimaced as he acknowledged his calls.

"Did you know that Mrs. Baxter was expecting and just had an abortion?"

Kimball hid his face in his hands, the great shoulders sagging. "Yes, I knew." The voice was muffled.

"You knew about the abortion?" Williams was intrigued.

"Yes, I paid for it. Wally was strapped for cash and I didn't want Darlene to know. She's so sensitive about abortions. All these years, she thinks that it's my fault we never had children. I had to protect her. You do see that don't you?" His dark eyes were pleading with them.

"Mr. Kimball, were the Baxter's aware of your concern for your wife?"

"Bette was."

"Were they blackmailing you for silence?"

"My God, no!" Kimball was outraged.

Williams decided it was too soon to take Kimball in. "Mr. Kimball, please stay in touch. We may need to ask further questions."

They started for the door, and Williams turned for one last question. "You wouldn't know why someone would want to kill them both?"

"I can't imagine anyone having reason enough to kill another human being."

Once they were outside, Don asked, "Why didn't we read him his rights and book him?"

"Where's your motive? Where's the weapon? Kimball would rather protect, not destroy. Blackmail would make him protect his wife. Let's see if we have enough to get a court warrant on his bank account based on his paying for the abortion."

"What about Mrs. Kimball? Is she really so naïve she didn't know what was happening?"

Williams considered. "Maybe, maybe not. Usually the wife is the last to know. Sometimes people in that age group prefer not knowing as a way to retain their lifestyle."

"Do we talk to her again?"

"Yes, we do."

The drive back to Snoqualmie Ridge was silent. The wooden greenery flashed by, broken by odd bits of open, rolling hills and clumps of homes and trailers. They took the Snoqualmie exit and headed back uphill.

Mrs. Kimball was surprised, yet managed to give the impression she was glad to see them. "Would you like some coffee and some brownies? I just baked them. They are Edward's favorite.

"No, thank you. We just wanted to ask a few more questions now that you've had a chance to calm down. Sometimes it helps to talk and you may be able to add a few details."

She sat like an obedient child, her hands folded demurely in her lap like a little girl waiting to give the correct answer to her teacher.

Detective Williams was annoyed. Who did she remind him of? She had a disconcerting way of looking at you, but never making eye contact.

"Do you bake often? His question was meant to put her at ease.

"Oh, my yes," she flushed with pleasure. "Edward does like home cooking, but he's so helpless in a kitchen. He couldn't find a pot to boil water in if he needed to. He needs me to take care of him."

Adler coughed. Williams shot him a warning glance. "I wondered if you could describe again how you found the Baxter's."

She lowered her head for a moment, took a deep breath, and began her recital. "I had a letter from our high school about our fortieth reunion. I went through the side gate to see if Bette was outside, it being so warm and such a good day for working in the flowers." She paused to draw a breath and consider. "They were just lying there on the lounges all stiff and cold. I remember being surprised at how much blood there was over them. It really was unexpected. Then I remembered how the chickens used to bleed whenever we butchered on the farm. Did you ever live on a farm?"

Her little girl voice mixed with her huge body was unsettling. I'm not really hearing her, Williams thought. He encouraged her rambling memory. "No, I didn't. Please go on."

"Well I knew I wasn't supposed to touch anything so I just went right home and called the police." She looked at him expectantly like a child silently asking validation for her actions.

"You didn't notice anything out of place?"

She shook her head. "No, nothing, of course, I didn't go inside."

"No trash strewn around? Something you might have picked up and brought home, then had Mr. Kimball haul it off to the transfer station?"

She looked at them blankly. "No, I did not touch anything. Besides, Mr. Kimball never takes anything to the transfer station. We have a disposal service, and the neighbor's son hauls yard clippings for us."

"Thank you, ma'am. We'll be in touch in case we need anything else."

In the car, he gave Adler instructions. "You're checking the Cedar Hills Drop Box and the Factoria Transfer Station personally. See if Kimball took in a load. The transfer station might have a license plate number or the camera has his arrival on record. You'll have to check out the digital record. Don't forget to describe him and his vehicle to the person in charge."

"What if he used someone else's vehicle?"

"Don't make problems."

Williams turned his mind inward. He was not pleased with the interview. If Kimball was so helpless in a kitchen, would he know how to use a knife? The Baxter's knives had all been there, neatly arranged in a wooden block. Mrs. Kimball would surely know if one were missing from her kitchen. Something she wouldn't mention if she were shielding Kimball. Probability? Mrs. Kimball would know which one was the butcher knife. The thought chilled him. Who did she remind him of? The answer was stored somewhere in the dark recesses of his mind waiting to be tapped. Williams never shrugged off similarities. The human condition has a proclivity for repetition.

Adler didn't have anything for three days. When he came into the office, he poured a cup of coffee and lowered himself into the extra chair. "I couldn't find anybody that remembered Kimball. I checked the camera's recording for three days afterward. Neither Kimball nor his vehicle were there."

Williams grimaced.

Adler continued. "So I went back to the neighborhood and checked with the teenagers to find the one who hauls off trash."

Williams refreshed his cup while listening.

"He's a nice kid that earns his money doing odd jobs. It seems Mrs. Kimball had a load of things from housecleaning to dispose of two days after the murder. Being a thrifty soul, she made sure several other neighbors had some things to send too. It cuts the individual price."

"Mrs. Kimball?"

Adler nodded.

William's lips tightened. "Let me guess. It was black, green, and grey trash sacks all mixed together."

"That's right. All neatly compacted at the transfer station and sent on to the landfill."

Williams clasped his hands and leaned forward on the desk. "Why did she kill them?"

Adler set the cup down. "Perhaps because of the affair. She's afraid of losing Kimball."

"She isn't though. She's quite confident he needs her."

"Maybe she knew about the baby and figured he'd leave this time." Adler refused to give ground.

"Why Walter Baxter too?"

"He was there."

"Why move the bodies? And where in the hell is that knife."

"It's probably in her garbage sack at the landfill, and I don't know why." Adler answered the last question first and then asked his own.

"All right, let's say Mrs. Kimball killed them, but she isn't acting like she hated Bette Baxter."

Williams sat back and grinned. "Pretty good. Now all we have to do is prove it beyond a reasonable doubt." He paused. "You're right, Mrs. Kimball is behaving differently, and she keeps reminding me of someone. I've been through the files of every homicide for the last ten years."

"Why?"

"Sometimes the knowledge of human quirks and how a human acts will give you an edge. It isn't only a matter of physical reaction," he continued at the raised eyebrows of the younger man. "Some people have a convoluted reason that makes sense to them. We need to lay a trap with bait."

"Won't the lawyers they will hire object?"

Williams slumped. "Do me a favor and describe Mrs. Kimball to me. Maybe something will click."

"Why? You've seen her. Why not describe her to someone who hasn't seen her?"

Williams shrugged. He knew Adler was right. He knew what Mrs. Kimball looked like and he couldn't connect her with that shadowy figure lurking in the background. If he hadn't gotten home so late the last few nights and Natty leaving so early for the morning painting classes, maybe he could have honed in on the answer. Natty could always straighten his thinking.

"You're right. "I want you to keep checking on Kimball. See where he goes in case we're wrong."

Williams watched the door close behind Adler and picked up the telephone to dial Natty.

Her husky, breathless voice was music in his ears. He hastily assured her that nothing was wrong and immediately launched into a description of Mrs. Kimball, including her little girl qualities. "Who does that remind you of?"

Her laugh gurgled over the line. "So that's why you called me. You just gave a perfect description of my mother's neighbor Doreen in her younger days. Remember, she murdered the girl who jilted her son. When the police arrested her son on suspicion of murder, she confessed. I'll never forget how she could give the appearance of being shy and withdrawn while edging so close, you'd have to move to find your own space."

Williams sighed. Leave it to Natty. She was still chattering. "Of course, after she got out of the institution, she tried to kill her son because he wouldn't let her live with him."

Williams tried not to be abrupt, but failed. "Thanks, Natty. I owe you a dinner, but I've got to run." He knew she was apt to start starching his underwear too as revenge. He'd really have to admire her paintings and attend that showing she scheduled next month to be forgiven.

He headed for Adler's cubicle. "We're going back to the Kimball's place."

Mrs. Kimball opened the door. Why, Detective Williams and Officer Adler, come in. Did you think of something else? Edward will be right out. He's shaving now." She motioned to the chairs.

"This is official, ma'am. We'll stand."

She looked perplexed. Mr. Kimball must have heard them and he appeared, freshly pink from a shave and definitely aggrieved by their intrusion.

Williams looked directly at him. "Mr. Kimball, you are under arrest for the murder of the Baxter's. Mrs. Kimball, you are under arrest as an accessory after the fact. We have a search warrant for this property. Officer Adler, read them their rights."

The reading was almost singsong, a tonal quality brought on with repetition, sounding like the prayers that kids once recited at school.

"Would you like to call your lawyer?" Williams asked when Adler finished.

"Yes," Kimball choked out the answer.

"Edward, don't be silly. You know you didn't murder them."

"Honey, that doesn't matter. They think I did."

Mrs. Kimball faced them as she took a half-step forward, her stout shoulders squared, and her hands on her hips.

"I'll not have this. Edward can't even bear to see me cut up the meat or clean fish. He couldn't possibly do anything like that."

"Yes, ma'am, if you'll be seated, Officer Adler will start the search."

"You don't believe me?"

"No, ma'am."

Her face crumpled and she hid behind her hands. Mr. Kimball put his arms around her, soothing her as a child. She took a deep breath and stood away, her pudgy features rearranged and determined. "I won't let you do this to Edward. He didn't kill them, you know. I did."

Adler stopped in mid-stride. Williams grunted. Kimball gulped, and then shouted. "Darlene, do not say another word. I'm calling Harrison."

"Oh, pooh, that fussbudget? Besides, Bette deserved it. She killed your baby."

Kimball's chin dropped. My God, thought Williams, he doesn't know he's been living with a murderer. Aloud, he said, "Mrs. Kimball, I warn you, anything you say can and will be held against you. Please, take your husband's advice." It was obvious she wasn't ignorant of the affair or its results.

Her shoulder slumped, just a fraction before she straightened again. "No, I did wrong. I'll have to be punished for that, but when I found the cancelled check for the abortion clinic, I knew that if I didn't punish Bette, no one would. I really thought that Wally was gone that night. He woke up, so I killed him too. I moved them outside so they wouldn't bleed all over the bed and carpet. After all, someone could use them again. The sheets and the knife I brought home, but the sheets smelled so from the blood, you know, I threw them in a garbage bag. The knife I cleaned and put back in the holder."

"You mean you've been using it?" Kimball looked ready to heave, choking on his own words and reflux.

"Why, of course, I have. It's a perfectly good knife. Though it did need a bit of sharpening right afterwards." She turned to Williams. "Do we go to the station now?" It was still a little girl's question.

* * *

Adler and Williams finished the reports on the Baxter's and decided to have one last cup of coffee. "Do you think the prosecution will be able to use her confession?"

Williams shrugged. "As long as she keeps on believing she has to be punished, her lawyer can't stop it. He could probably plead insanity in her case."

"You were never convinced that Kimball did it, were you? Why?"

"Mrs. Kimball grew up on a farm in Iowa. It's usually the farm women who kill and butcher the chickens. She just forgot about all the blood and said so. Kimball is perplexed over the idea of killing, let alone actually committing one. She reminded me of a murderer and Kimball didn't."

"Do you think he'll stick by her?"

Williams considered his mother-in-law's neighbors. "He probably will until after the trial, maybe."

"How could you be so certain that she would confess?"

Williams described the similarity between the two murderers. "Both were oversized people with a little girl's possessiveness and both had the ability to intrude into another's territory without seeming to do so. Just remember where the human condition is concerned, the French are right: The more things change, the more they remain the same.

Skogfru

"We are going to clean private, neglected property. We are not endangering the wilderness, nor are we abdicating our stand for code enforcement in this community."

I kept my voice under control, allowing no anger to escape. I rolled my eyes at Jerry who was trying not to giggle. Two hundred pound men shouldn't giggle, should they?

"So sue us!" I shouted into the phone before hitting the End button.

"Damn, damn, and damn. Now they are going to picket." I pushed a stray strand of hair back into the general direction of my ponytail.

"Why sue us?" Jerry's words rumbled past his beard.

"They won't. They'll have to sue the town of Hopewell and the National Registry. They gave us the permission to take out the undergrowth. This group wants the property left in its unspoiled state, quote, and unquote."

I stood and reached for the tea. "Just what we need: A bunch of half-cocked, unheard of environmentalists."

"Who?"

"This group calls themselves Earth's Loving Friends. Their acronym is ELFS. They are more like gremlins or trolls, if you ask me.

"Trolls were my grandmother's favorite way of quelling youthful exuberance. Horrid wood trolls, the dark elves with stumpy tails, which could put you forever in their power if you said yes to one of their questions. If you cut a branch off their dwelling place, you must ask their permission."

"But that was in Sweden, not Western Washington."

"They are like the Tommy Knockers and immigrated according to my grandmother."

"What are Tommy Knockers?"

"They're Welsh mining elves. They are said to knock when danger is in the mine."

His education in folklore was interrupted by the shrilling telephone. I motioned to Jerry to take it and fled for the bathroom. One more complaint about restoring the old Langdorf orchard and I would scream.

I studied my face in the mirror. The features were still the same. Nothing extraordinary framed by a red-gold mass of hair disengaging from the ponytail. It was time to redo it. I braided it into a long rope before walking out.

Jerry looked up from the desk. "No sweat, boss lady. One client wanted to make sure we are on the job Monday morning, someone wants a bid for a small condo landscape, the local blab wants to take our picture while we are returning Langdorf's place to a thing of beauty, and the Scouts will be there at nine o'clock."

"Thank God. Jerry, do you realize how important this project is? One or two of those old trees might produce varieties now unknown or forgotten. We're working with living history. We might even be able to donate to the National Center for Genetic Resources in Fort Collins, Colorado.

"Then you'd become famous, right?"

"Wrong. Most people won't know or care, but I will." I glanced out the window.

"If this rain would have stopped last month we could have been in there already. No one would have made a big deal about a few Boy and Girl Scouts picking up trash."

"True, but you should have consulted the great Western Washington Weather Gods."

I laughed. Jerry could do that, that and all the heavy work involved in being landscape designers.

"Are we ready for tomorrow?"

"Yep, all the chainsaws are primed and raring to chew."

"Is Balantine ready with the sprayer?"

"He's all set to go." Jerry replied.

"The spraying for fungus should really give the ELFS fits. They want us to restore thirty years of neglect organically. No matter, we'll meet there at six." Jerry and I might spend an occasional night together, but our lives were separate.

Six o'clock in Western Washington on an April morning can cause difficulties with perception as to where the sky begins and the mist ends. This Saturday was no exception. The mist drifted lazily downward. It was insufficient to soak through clothing, but enough to mix with one's sweat and thoroughly drench the body within two hours. We cut and stacked fallen timbers, cut away the dead branches, and sealed the cuts on the apple, pear, and cherry trees. They, like the original fauna, had gone wild.

"Too bad the season is so late. I can't do any proper pruning until fall." Jerry nodded at the trees. "We can't even get to the last acre until we clear the brush. You'd think somebody in the estate would have cared enough to hire a gardener."

"They live in Europe. I guess they forgot how fast salmon berries grow.

"When is Balantine due?" I changed the subject.

"He said he be here by eleven o'clock. That gives the urchins time to work."

Three stations wagons were arriving. I looked at my watch. Five minutes past nine. The Scouts were right on time. Young uniformed people began piling out of the vehicles. The larger uniforms were handing out gloves and trash bags. One made his way over.

"I'm Scout Master Dave Bentley." His hand was extended.

"Welcome, my name is Lynn Helgason and this is my associate Jerry Vale." We all shook hands.

"Just have them get the trash where we cleared. Don't try to get through all the brambles to the last acre."

The small uniforms had spread out and were busy picking up the litter from forgotten beer busts and blown in trash.

"Careful, don't cut yourselves," shouted one of the full-sized uniforms.

The reporter and photographer arrived, one with her note pad, the other with her camera. She was already busy snapping the young people. I hurried over to greet them; relieved that the ELFS hadn't arrived.

I should have shelved that thought. Around the corner appeared an old bus painted green and brown and emblazoned with orange lettering. It pulled up next to the reporter's SUV and blocked any exit. A motley crew of long hair, beards, and tattered rags spilled out of the bus.

"They must think it's the sixty's," Jerry muttered.

It took time to sort them out, but one was older, her long, grey hair hung past her shoulders and her taupe face was wrinkled. Her lean body was wrapped in a brown burlap cape that floated almost to the ground. Her widow's peak gave an owl like look to the huge, dark eyes under busy, grey eyebrows. Those eyes drew my attention. They were deep-set and were filled with pain and distrust. She spat on the ground after slowly examining us. The others stood behind her, waiting for her to move or speak. She folded her arms across her chest and studied the activity of the Scouts.

I was still clutching my Stihl chainsaw like a weapon. The reporter was busy taking notes, the photographer was snapping pictures, and the Scout Master and one Den Mother were rounding up their charges.

"Don't get near them," hissed the Den Mother.

She then turned to me. "I never really cared for your life style since you moved here, but compared to you, these people are complete sleazes." Was this acceptance by the community for a woman who ran a man's business?

"You'll have to move that bus." The well-fed Scout Master was giving an order.

That prompted a conference. The older woman must have seen the futility of frightening children. Harmless victims would not win them support and a skinny male got in and backed out the bus.

The Scouts cleared out. They'd left their filled and half-filled bags for later pickup. They had earned their Community Badges.

The marchers settled in for a day of walking and chanting, their green and beige capes slapping and swirling around red, chapped legs. After giving the reporter our names, business name, and address, Jerry and I attacked the fallen branches and salmon berries. We ate lunch in his pickup, each side ignoring the other.

Ballantine was only two hours late. He arrived at one o'clock, waved at the marchers, and handed Jerry two sprayers.

"Outnumbered," he mumbled through thin lips and returned to his pickup. He sped down the road while the ELFS jeered at him.

Jerry looked at me. "We might as well save the spraying until tomorrow. If we're lucky, the mist will be gone."

"Be sure you lock them in the truck, but you're right. We can't spray now."

The mist kept coming as we advanced against the undergrowth. Every year blackberry brambles had shot out branches twenty to thirty feet. The roots had grown as thick as my forearm. The salmonberries' and thimbleberries' branches waved over our heads and had interlaced their roots underground effectively pushing aside and choking any legitimate garden growth. We did not dare spray root killer for the fruit trees were too valuable and too fragile from years of neglect. We bent, and pulled, heaved and tossed. By nightfall we were soaked through.

The ELFS left as we cleaned our gear and stowed it.

"Maybe it will clear tomorrow," Jerry offered.

"Hah!"

"They've soured your disposition. I'll be out early in the morning, but then I have to go to Gram's house for her birthday."

"Right." I yawned. Every muscle in my neck and shoulders ached. I longed for the shower.

"Did you notice the Native American woman?"

"I couldn't miss her. Why, Jerry?"

"I don't know. She just seemed different. Not angry like the rest. Just sad. What tribe lived around here?"

"An offshoot of the Sammamish would be my guess, but they left early in the nineteenth century. This place was built about 1870."

"Huh, anyway, I'll start the burning in the morning as per the permit. Think you can handle it alone?"

"No problem, Jerry, only their mouths are vicious." We went our separate ways.

The next morning was different. The grey skies were still there, but the mist was gone. Just the clouds and humidity remained. It's the type of climate where sixty degrees feels like you are working in eighty degrees. The ELFS were there to greet us, booing as we drove up. When we started spraying, they started swinging their huge signs and wailing like banshees.

"Damn them!" I was angry again. "Why can't they see that we are bringing something back to life? Why didn't they stay in the ground and emerge in the moonlight like normal elves?"

Jerry grinned. "Not letting it get to you, are you?"

"I guess I am. It's like they are threatening everything I've worked to accomplish. I've always needed to grow new life, bring back what was once productive." I stopped. I was starting to ramble.

"You're right, Jerry, it's time to work. Ignore them."

Once the fungus spraying was done, we returned to the drudgery of clearing brush. Cut away the brambles that waved over our heads, pull, heave, and dig at the stubborn roots, and then add it all to the fire. We broke once for tea. You would have thought the ELFS would be bored. Instead they kept up their insane chant and shuffling march. The old woman did not march. She stood silently, regarding us with baleful eyes. Sorrow had etched new lines in her face.

"Maybe I shouldn't leave you alone here."

"Don't worry about it. There is only seven of them counting the old woman."

"I'll talk to them before I leave."

Just as he said, Jerry spoke to the lanky man at the head of the procession. They exchanged heated words. It sounded like he suggested what Jerry could do to himself. Jerry forgot he was outnumbered and answered back. Whatever he said made the lanky man angry and he swung.

Jerry decked him. The man hit the ground, his nose splattered against his face, his blood fertilizing the apple tree.

"Revenge, revenge! Great Mother, hear us." Two of the women were jumping and making a flapping circle around Jerry. The old woman walked over and knelt beside the man.

"Do you now despoil men along with the Earth?" She asked as she looked up at Jerry.

Jerry had his shoulders hunched, his head lowered to his chest, and his fists were bunched as he waited for another attack. "Self-protection," he grunted, his eyes going from ELF to ELF.

She remained on her knees and considered. "That is true. He swung first. What did you say to him?"

"Not half of what he said to me." Jerry's anger had flushed his face almost to the color of his beard. "I just told him no rough stuff while I was gone, and to insure that, you people were leaving now."

The old woman stood before speaking. "You are leaving?"

"I was."

She turned to the others who had formed a chanting circle around us. "The rest of you take him to our healing spot and return to me this evening." She turned to Jerry.

"When they are gone, you too can leave. Or are you afraid to leave her with me?"

Jerry stared at her. I could detect no mockery in her voice. It was a gentle, sensible voice with a slight quaver common to the elderly although her movements were not those of the extreme aged. We stepped back as four of the ELFS picked up the prone body and carried the man to the bus.

"Sit him upright so that he does not choke on his own blood," she admonished them.

Quiet descended on our ears. It was a relief not to hear the continual chant.

"You need not worry. They will not return to me until this evening."

Jerry was like a puzzled bull that lost sight of the matador. There was no one left to hook or gore. First he would look at her and then at me.

"You go ahead, Jerry. Your family is expecting you. I don't want to alienate your grandmother."

"Are you sure you will be okay?"

"Of course."

He leaned toward me and gave me a light kiss on the cheek. He did not have to bend. I'm that tall. He touched my shoulder lightly.

"See you." With that, he stepped into his truck and left.

The elderly woman and I eyed each other. How old was she? It was difficult to tell. Her movements were quick, but the voice quavered, and the grey hair, the wrinkles, the sorrowful eyes gave no real answer.

"I am Alice Skougman."

Surprise must have shown on my face for she gave a slight shrug and continued. "We do not use Native American names. My surname is from my father, an immigrant from Sweden. He, too, cut the trees. He was vain like all mortal men and could not feel the sap flowing in them."

There is no answer for such a statement. I simply nodded and introduced myself. "I'm Lynn Helgason. Why don't we call a truce and eat lunch together?" I had read somewhere that if you eat with an enemy they would become your friend. I doubted it, but at least she would not be chanting with her mouth full.

We sat on the tailgate. Not a word passed between us while we ate. Our music was the songs from the birds that nested in the old orchard and the busy sound of scurrying, small animals. Alice kept her shawl firmly around her shoulders.

"Why do you do this?" She waved her arm towards the trees and the cleared pathways.

"It is to bring alive something that was dying; to restore them to their original grandeur. By doing this, I'm part of something ancient and worthwhile.

This time she really looked at me, wonderment growing on her face. "Don't you realize that you are destroying the homes and food of the little ones?"

I thought of the little warbler that had scolded me as I cleared away a tangle of berry brambles. His little olive green wings almost shook, and the little yellow throat throbbed with indignation.

"We are only clearing to the end of the orchard. There will still be plenty of bushes and brambles down the bank and along the creek."

"Do you really expect the brush to stay there? In a few years your work will be undone."

"We're collecting funds for a fence and upkeep. Someday there will be a regular gardener, and people will come to see their heritage. They will be able to eat the fruits that their ancestors ate." I noticed the grey hair floating in wisps over her shoulders. She seemed very old and vulnerable.

She shook her head. "All growing things are ancient." Her dark eyes seemed to grow larger. "Are you not planning to put out poison for the shrews and moles that gnaw away at the roots, the rodents that eat the bark, and the deer that nibble at the shoots? And will the poison not kill others not intended to die?"

"The trees here are old enough that we aren't worried about the bark or the roots. No, no poison is planned. We do have to spray for disease and fungus, but that should not hurt the birds or the animals."

She shook her head and lowered it to her chest.

"I need to get back to work." I wiped my hands and returned everything to the cab, leaving her there in her sorrow and silence.

First I stirred the fire before adding fern fronds and blackberry brambles. The mist had started again, but the fire was hot enough to continue burning.

By two o'clock the mist lifted and a slight breeze drove me back to the burn pile to make sure no stray embers would blow out. I kept adding debris and roots. It was becoming quite a trudge from the back of the lot to the front where we had permission to burn. The old woman's sorrow had been like a shadow on my spirits. She never bothered me, never interfered, and had not chanted. She just stood there like some half-wild creature staring at my frenetic efforts. I took time to pour a cup of tea from the thermos and gather my strength for next assault.

"You are weary from your labors."

"I've only today left to clear this. Tomorrow it is business as usual."

The sun broke through the clouds leaving a hole of brilliant blue overhead. In the west the white clouds were gathering into a sullen grey. Any respite from the mist would not be long.

"While there is light, why not walk with me and see what lives and eats here?" Alice nodded at the land.

"I'm quite cognizant of the local fauna." I had not meant to be so curt, but I was tired.

"Do you really know them all?"

"Yes," I snapped back.

She smiled, the creases deepening in her face, but it was her eyes that held me; deep black, vibrating with electricity that swirled between us as the Earth became alive. I could hear the chirps, tweets, fluttering and bustle of the land around us.

"Come," she commanded softly. "I will show you, but step lightly. We will not disturb those who make their home here."

We walked to the shrub filled section in silence. The branches and brambles parted to give us room. She lovingly touched the pink blossoms of the salmonberries. "How the rufous-sided towhee love these. It is part of their food and drink."

I could only nod. Who hasn't seen them eating the fruit in the wilds?

"And these." Her fingers brushed the budding thimbleberry in a blessing. "To humans they are bland, but the huge brown one comes down from high to feed on them."

Her hand stopped me while her eyes searched among the roots. "There." She pointed to a depression lined with leaves. "Man calls that dweller a warbler. Some say Wilson's, others Wood. It does not matter. They feast on insects. What will your spray do to them?"

She drew me towards the small stream where alders and willows fight with the cottonwood to spread their limbs outward and upward. Red elderberry and ferns fought for their own space, and underneath the creeping blackberry vines tore at my pants.

"See," she pointed to the belted kingfisher swishing down to claim his prey.

"And there." She pointed to an opening on the opposite bank. "If you wait, quietly and long enough, you will see the red furred one. He is powerful for such a small one."

I blinked, straining to delve through the earth for any movement within. My head was fuzzy from the tweeting of the birds, their songs blending into a chant that lulled my mind. Bees hummed from bush to bush, hurrying before the rain and cool clouds made them listless again.

"Come, there is still much to see and hear." Her voice was soft, luring me on. "Do you hear the songs of the little ones?"

"Yes, clearly."

Again she favored me with that wondrous smile and her face became young, and she was beautiful. "When you truly listen, you can hear the songs of the trees. Not the sounds of their outgrowing leaves, but the sound of their souls as the sap flows through them, nourishing all those around and in them."

Before I would have laughed, but now I did not. Somehow laughter had become inappropriate.

She led me back to a fallen log near the bank. It had once been a mighty cedar, perhaps a victim of the vicious winds that howl in the winter. It had grown soft and rotted, held firm by the heavy moss coating its length.

"See," she commanded as she pointed at the end snagged away from the ground, its old roots covered with lighter-green colored lichen. Part of its base was bared and shattered, huge chunks torn away. "The redhead has been here. Look closely at its old home where its life was torn from the ground. There more life finds shelter."

In the moss lined cavity were six white eggs, stippled with reddish brown. She pulled me away and sprinkled leaves and twigs in our footprints. "The wren is very timid." She led me to the other end of the trunk and pointed to the ground.

"Now I am tired. Do you mind if we rest?"

She sat on the ground, leaning her shoulders into the wood. I sat beside her, weary in bone and mind. I did not wish to argue any of her views. Some were valid, but I loved the old orchard.

Alice gazed at the clouds grouping and forming above us. "It smells good here."

Again my answering yes wreathed her face in a smile, but it was true. The earth, the mosses, the trees, the bracken, the early blossoms, all had a scent of their own. They blended in the light breeze and became part of the air. It was pleasant to rest and feel the loosening of muscle and bone. The silence wasn't really silence, for the small ones, as she called them, continued their busy chatter, and I could speak again.

"I'm surprised your friends haven't returned."

"They are not my friends. They are my children."

"But they are so different." I felt guilty of some crime for saying that. Perhaps they were her children in spirit.

Her voice became a crooning whisper. "Oh, their fathers were all men, but they are my children. They are my children of the wood."

The last of the sun was sealed away by the waiting clouds. The air carried by the wind was soft and sweet, bringing the sky's grayness to my eyes.

"Rest now for you are weary."

Was she really crooning a lullaby that mingled with the melody of the leaves? Too late I remembered the name Skougman. They are the wood folk, the dark elves called skogfru in my grandparents' Sweden. They trap your soul when you answer yes to one of their questions.

Even this knowledge cannot rouse me for her voice is now my grandmother's voice and I am part of the earth that I rest upon.

Did I really waken enough to see her pull the moss from the old tree trunk and spread its protective warmth over me? I cannot remember. The songs of the birds, the clatter of the woodpecker's bill all mingle with the earth's vibrations and I am growing, and my roots are deep.

The Imitators

Paula Kingman was led from her cement cell, through the grey hall to a small room done in faux stone. Faux wood chairs sat on either side of a wooden desk. There was another door on the other side of the desk. Her prison uniform was a dull yellow and the yellowed lighting cast a harsh yellow glare over her and the chair facing the desk and other door.

The man sitting at the desk was wearing a vivid teal blue suit. His hair was straight and black; his nose and lips as thin as his body. His face sported a tan, proving that he either took vacations in the sunny part of the world or he could afford the tanning dens. His cold eyes matched the color of his suit.

"You are to sit in the other chair. If you do not answer correctly, I decide your punishment. You will then be given time to dwell on your answers and we will meet again tomorrow. Frankly, I do not wish another session with you.

"Now, you are to tell me when the transfer took place."

Paula's insides shrank at the man's words. She had no idea what transfer he meant. All she knew was that last night the officers appeared at her dorm room, arrested her, secured her mouth and wrists, threw her into the back of an ovoid transporter, and handed her over to the prison clerks and guards. There was no advocate, and from the prison workers, no information. They refused to speak to her. She had been stripped and photographed; probed by scanners and poked with needles. She was given a hideous uniform that bagged on her slender frame. Her cell had a small washstand and commode, no towels, and no bedding. She'd spent the night shivering. The morning food was some sort of tasteless paste squeezed out of a tube into her mouth. She welcomed the warmth in this room, but this was an Inquisitor Jurist; referred to in the media as IQJ. His power over her fate was absolute, and his question made no sense. How was she to answer him?

"Come, come, answer me." His voice was impatient. "Do you think those large brown eyes of yours or your perfect features will distract me? We are aware of how such attractions are used to distort our perceptions of your character."

Paula wet her lips. "Please, sir, I don't know what transfer you mean. I don't even know why I'm here."

He glared at her. "When did you become Paula Kingman? What happened to the real Paula?"

"But I am Paula Kingman. It's the name my parents gave me."

He leaned forward; his strange eyes looking directly at her while his right index finger beat a tattoo on the black circles on the desk. The circles began to emit a black glow that cast eerie shadows over his angular face.

"When you requested clearance for the experiments in the chemical lab, you had to submit to a blood test. Why were you so foolish? The proof is right here. You are not human. You are an Imitator from elsewhere. We need to know where you are from and why you and your ilk are here. Why are you infiltrating our government and our populace? We will not let you eliminate us."

Paula's mouth had lowered and her eyes widened. "I, I don't understand. I had no reason not to submit to a blood test. I was assigned to the University and required to take the blood test for the assigned project. I cannot serve the State if I do not graduate."

The man straightened. "We are at this moment interviewing all of your known acquaintances and evaluating everything from your living quarters. You are to stop these prevarications and tell me your real identity, the names of your contacts, where you make your informational drops, and the ultimate goal of the Imitators. You will be banished from society, but you will live if you cooperate."

Paula swallowed before speaking. "Please, sir, I have no contacts. I am who I say I am. I've never been anywhere except to my assigned classes. If the class was scheduled for a visit to a museum or science center for enlightenment, I went with my class."

"Since you are being uncooperative, I'll start with basic questions.

"How old are you?"

"I'm twenty-five, sir."

"What year were you born?"

"2643."

"What month and day?" A slight frown whipped across his face as this was 2668.

"Dragon the seventh."

"And, of course, we'll find your birth papers at your quarters."

"Yes, sir, I've always kept those with me. Mrs. Gooding stressed how important that was for an orphan."

His face became bland and his eyes brightened. "Who is Mrs. Gooding? Where will we find her?"

"She is the lady that ran the Family Home I was sent to when my parents were killed. I presume she is still in the same house. I've not been back there since the government assigned me to the University and issued me quarters there. The work has been too intense, and I have no money to take a trip."

"Where was this home? I need the address and the Sector."

"It is, or was, at 21888 SE 248th, in the Bloom Sector."

"How old were you when you left?"

"I was eighteen, sir. That is the prescribed age for terming out of parental care." Her husky voice was quite prim. Surely, the man must know that.

"How old were you when your parents died?"

"I was five as I had not started regular school."

"How did both of your parents die?"

"It was a vehicular collision. They had left me in the care of a neighbor while they went to a government music performance."

"How do you remember that?"

"I was on the front stoop waving goodbye when they rose in the air. Another vehicle came hurtling through the trees and struck them. It was horrible. Both vehicles exploded in flames. I screamed then and for years would wake up screaming from the dreams of my parents being burned."

"Mrs. Gooding then became your second mother, is that correct?"

"No, not really. There were always six of us living in her house. She was fair, but not demonstrative. She followed all the rules and prepared us to live according to our assignments. We always had our chores and our homework."

"When did Mrs. Gooding give you the birth records?"

"They were in my box that the government gave her after cleaning out my parents' home. The records stayed in my box and that was kept in the room I shared with another girl."

"Do you still have that box?"

"Yes, sir, it is in my quarters." She noticed his eyes had become very bright.

"What was your original address?"

"I don't remember. I don't know if I ever knew it."

"Would Mrs. Gooding have it?"

"I don't know, sir."

"Who is your Medical Provider?"

"I don't have one. I've not been ill, not really. Mrs. Gooding took us all in for our vaccinations, but that was years ago. I have been to the University medical center whenever I had a bad cold. They prescribed a decongestant."

"What about birth prevention?"

Paula blushed. "I haven't dated anyone. I, I never met anyone outside of the school sector and there are no transportation chits for us."

"Do you expect me to believe that you, an Imitator with quite good features and figure, have never been with a male? Why are you here if not to propagate?"

Paula's eyes showed bewilderment. "I am to study diligently to serve the State. Mrs. Gooding and our instructors explained that we are forever indebted for the care and schooling we received. All the education courses required that I sign for the amounts due once I am employed. The forms emphasize how we are forever in the State's debt."

The IQJ frowned. "Your answers have not helped the situation. You must realize that humans can live for a few weeks without food, but cannot live any length of time without water. We don't know if the Imitators are the same. They, however, seem to die more agonizing deaths. Quite fascinating to watch. I don't suppose you have watched any of our executions."

"No! Never!"

"We are verifying the information that you have given us. If just one statement is incorrect, I'll sentence you to be repeatedly raped before you are sent into isolation to die by deprivation. If, by some small chance, you have answered truthfully, you will be placed in isolation away from real people. If I choose the execution, I shall enjoy watching." His smile radiated satisfaction.

"We will meet again tomorrow. Until then you are permitted food and water. You may now thank me for my generosity."

Paula's face was white. She wanted to destroy him, scratch his eyes out, but years of training forced the words out.

"Thank you, sir."

She heard the door open and a guard yanked her roughly to her feet.

"Return that creature to her cell. She is allowed food and water until tomorrow."

The IQJ pressed one of the black buttons as they left the room. "Have you arrested Mrs. Gooding?"

"Yes, sir, she is now in custody and on her way here. We're testing her blood again, although according to her medical recs, she had one last year. There are no prior records of an Imitator residing there."

"Is she still caring for young girls?"

"Yes, sir, a competent matron has been put in charge and every one of the residents and employees are being tested. Did you want them sent to you?"

"Only if they are Imitators, however, I do expect Mrs. Gooding to be brought in and thoroughly investigated." He frowned at the circles.

"What about the accident she described killing her so-called parents?"

"We've verified that one occurred in the Bloom Sector in 2648. We are now checking the records of the people who died. Some of those records, however, were lost due to changing technologies, and quite frankly, sir, sloppy record keeping."

"I will allot you twenty hours to procure the needed information. I will need it tomorrow before eight. If it was her 'parents,'" he sneered over the word, "I want their birth, employment and acquaintance records also."

The IQJ pushed another circle for the next accused.

* * *

Paula was led back into the same room the next morning. There were now two chairs on her side and one was occupied by a dark-haired woman whose back looked familiar. She sat in her chair, stiff and ready. Her food had been nothing but a plain gruel with a half-way soured milk. Something must have been in the milk for she felt woozy. The door on the other side opened and the same IQJ appeared. He took the seat across from them. His suit today was a brilliant red and on his face a tight, satisfied smile as he looked at them.

"Well, it seems your reunion is less than joyous."

Paula blinked her eyes. Reunion? With who? She cautiously turned her head toward the other woman and gave a short gasp as she recognized Mrs. Gooding.

"What, no words of greeting between you? I would have thought, you, Mrs. Gooding, would give some sort of acknowledgement to your prize pupil."

"I had no prize pupil, sir, as no form of favoritism is allowed. It would have caused problems."

His eyes narrowed. "Do you deny that shortly after this Imitator arrived at your house you had the wherewithal to purchase a plush apartment in Old York?"

Paula continued to switch her gaze between the two. Old York was the art, fashion, and entertainment center of the Bloom Sector, a place where only the wealthy could afford to live.

"I, I don't know what you mean. I did purchase an apartment shortly after Paula was assigned to my care, but that was purchased from my savings and a small inheritance from an aunt. I bought an apartment for the day I could no longer fulfill my obligation to the State by caring for bereft girls."

The teal eyes hardened. "You were given Veracity. Why are you lying? You are to tell me immediately who contacted you. Was it her so-called parents?"

Mrs. Gooding seemed to shrink back in her chair. "I don't know who it was. They never gave me a name."

"So it was a man and woman."

Paula could hear Mrs. Gooding's heavy breathing. "No, sir, it was two men. They said all I had to do was sign papers and the place was mine. They insisted all new arrivals must be treated the same. I, I thought they were from the State."

The man's hard face became sterner. "You don't expect me to believe you are that simple. I want decent answers. What were their names?"

"I don't remember."

He touched a black circle and two guards stepped in.

"Mrs. Gooding, for your lies, your deceptions, for taking bribes from the Imitators, and for depriving the State of needed information, you are hereby judged. The sentence is death. Before you are destroyed, you will be questioned by a higher Inquisitor. I suggest you answer correctly or the Veracity will slowly disintegrate your body. Either way, your death will be quite painful and it will be shown on the evening entertainment. Your actions almost paved the way for an Imitator to enter our society.

"Take her out, now."

"No!" Mrs. Gooding was screaming. "Please, I really don't remember their names. They were slender, well dressed men like..." Her voice faltered as the guards dragged a wailing Mrs. Gooding away

"You may have realized that as an Imitator, you have already been given Veracity. In fact, it was administered the first day. Do you know how and why Veracity works?"

"Yes, sir, chemistry is part of my major. The drug reacts to the hormones and enzymes your own system produces. Lies produce certain enzymes which triggers the process of slowly destroying one's vital organs. However, it is believed that any stressful situation can bring on the same reactions. An antidote is usually given should the suspect be proven innocent."

"You have not been given an antidote. You are an Imitator of human life and will never be given one. This situation has to have been stressful, yet your body shows no symptoms."

"I am still young, sir. The process takes longer." Paula tried desperately to remain calm, but inside her stomach was knotted. She wished to be far, far away from her tormentor.

He leaned forward. "In fact, you have not shown much in the way of emotion except bewilderment at being here. You showed no grief over Mrs. Gooding's coming death."

"Mrs. Gooding was always a caretaker, nothing else. She rarely smiled at us. Her entire household was sterile. Any girl there was thrilled to leave. As for my behavior, I am still bewildered, sir. I have never done anything against the State and never will. I am most grateful for the opportunities I have been given. The University that I am attending is one of most prestigious in the land."

The IQJ glared at her. "The assignment was based on your grades and your IQ tests before your true status was known. We are left with a problem. We do not know if Veracity works the same in an Imitator as in a human. The others died rather than be taken. You have not committed any crimes against the State other than exist. You did not resist arrest and you have stated you will never do anything against the State. Does that mean you will notify us when you are contacted?"

For a moment, Paula's face was blank. Was he going to let her live?

"Why, yes, of course, I would notify you." She hesitated. "Do you mean I am to notify you directly? How would I do that, sir?"

"No, I do not mean you notify me. You will be given instructions when back on campus by people who will look like normal students. You are to walk each evening in the park. If you don't notify us and the Veracity works, your death will be slow and you will not be allowed medical treatment. To maintain a controlled observation, you will be permitted to return to your studies."

Paula's eyes widened and she took in a deep breath of air.

"The professor at the Lab will monitor your condition. Your absence in class will be noted as an illness and they are monitoring you for the effects of a new drug. We presume the Imitators will contact you before you graduate. Once you graduate the court will review all records and decide where and how to place you. You are not permitted to leave the campus complex unless under guard. Do you understand these conditions?"

"Yes sir, your honor, thank you." Paula was shaking. Her life would be no different than it had been.

"Since the University contains all that a small Sector contains, you won't be living a life of deprivation. Remember, we will know when someone contacts you." He pushed a circle and one of the guards entered.

"You are to take her back to the origins room. Her clothing and personal effects are to be returned. She is to be escorted under guard to the University and she is to arrive there in perfect condition. All charges are held in abeyance."

Paula's hands shook as she dressed and accepted her pack and PID card. She sat quietly, hardly daring to breathe until they landed at the

University and personnel signed her back in with a reminder that the medical unit prescribed a walk every evening.

The first thing she did when returning to quarters was to shower. It was a symbolic washing away of the smells and horror of her confinement. Not that the décor here was much different, but blankets, personal items, and blue school uniforms added a bit of color. She hurried to the cafeteria and ate her first real meal in two days. It didn't matter that the protein patty had been over cooked and the cheese a pasty imitation—it was food. She decided to do an early evening walk as tomorrow would be a full day of classes and study. All walking would be at night.

The woodland park consisted of two acres (precisely measured) of trees bordered by hedges and benches. An occasional bird would appear, sometimes even nest, although that was rare. The leaves offered shade in summer and the evergreens color in winter. Paula had not frequented the trails often. She preferred to study. With a shock, she realized two young men, dressed in the blue school uniform had appeared on each side of her, matching her every step. They both nodded and gave her a quick smile before the dark haired one spoke.

"We are to take the next path and walk directly to the small block building at the end. The door will open for us. There is a tunnel that will take you to your meeting."

"Are you my contacts for the State?"

"That will be explained by the next person you see. We will not meet again, nor will we speak until inside the building."

It took ten minutes to walk the distance and as they approached the door swung open.

Inside the brown haired one offered her a vial.

"It is the antidote."

Paula stared at him. His features were regular, his eyes friendly, and he appeared to be about her age. "How, uh, an antidote to what?"

"I wasn't told." He smiled at her again. "This way we really don't know, but it was suggested you take it immediately. We aren't sure of how strong drugs and poisons act in our system."

Paula frowned and stared at the vial. Was this a trick? Was this really an antidote? "What do you mean 'in our system'?"

"You were given the answer yesterday."

"How do I know you are telling the truth?"

"You'll just have to trust us," said the other one and slid back a panel. "I suggest you take it now and then go down this tunnel. When we leave, the outside door will lock and will not unlock until you've spoken to the person you are to meet."

"Don't you know I'll report you?"

Their faces grew stern. "Your report will be based on your meeting. Now go quickly, we want to close this panel." He handed her a light. The two of them took her arms when she didn't move and shoved her inside before closing the panel behind her.

Paula whirled and banged her fist on the panel, but it did not move. She was angry: angry at the world, at her dead parents, and at herself. She looked at the vial in her hand. Surprisingly, it had not broken. Is this some sort of new plastic? Or is this some sort of technology brought in by the Imitators? What if it killed her? Paula no longer cared. The last two days had been so bizarre, so unsettling that a sense of fatalism washed over her.

Her world had been turned upside down again. Her parents had been loving and caring. They provided her with a secure world. Then it was ripped away. Mrs. Gooding had been cold, uncaring, but at least secure. Now everything was wrong. Who and what was she if not human? She would meet the creature at the end. She swallowed the liquid, squared her chin, lifted the light and marched onward. If this killed her, at least the torment would end.

The tunnel was like much of this crammed together world: grey cement. Someone must use it frequently, she decided. It was swept clean and smelled slightly of fresh air. The tunnel crept downward and curved almost to a ninety degree angle before ending abruptly at a faux (she was certain it was fake) wooden panel. She shoved against it and entered the room. A man was standing at the far end of the small room waiting for her.

He smiled and his teal blue eyes were no longer cold, but glowing with pride. "Welcome, my dear, you were superb!

Stunned, Paula looked at him while the man continued speaking.

"Your parents sacrifice has been justified. You are perfectly positioned to infiltrate the scientific resources of this planet. Within a few years, this planet will belong to us."

"Now to specifics; you will report the two young men as contacts to your Counselor. She will assume the ones in the Woods delivered the message. Later, when we place you in a prestigious position, you will learn who the real contacts are. The two young men will not be found.

"You will now return the way you came. We realize you are confused, but this room will not exist if you try to report me; nor will they believe you. I suggest you hurry or be trapped underground."

He smiled, pushed a different panel, entered as the panel slid back into place behind him, and Paula was left alone in the room.

About the Author

Mari Collier lives in the quirky, little (technically) city of Twentynine Palms. It is home to the largest Marine Training Base in the United States. There are numerous art galleries, beauty/barber shops, and a fantastic little theater. She is a Director on the Board of the Twentynine Palms Historical Society, Coordinator of the Desert Writers Guild, and Congressional Secretary for Good Shepherd Lutheran Church.

Website: http://www.maricollier.com/